BALLER BOYS

Venessa Taylor

Published in Great Britain by Hashtag Press 2020

Text copyright © Venessa Taylor 2020
Illustrations copyright © Kenneth Ghann 2020
Cover Design © Helen Braid 2020

A CIP catalogue for this book is available from the British Library.

ISBN 978-1-9162864-0-5

Typeset in Calibri 12.25/16 by Blaze Typesetting
Printed in Great Britain by Clays Ltd, Elcograf S.p.A.

Hashtag PRESS
HASHTAG PRESS BOOKS
Hashtag Press Ltd
Kent, England, United Kingdom
Email: info@hashtagpress.co.uk
Website: www.hashtagpress.co.uk
Twitter: @hashtag_press

In loving memory of my late son-in-law Reece Darcheville. This is the book you asked me to write, I hope I've done you proud.

Acknowledgements

This book would not have been written without the help and support of countless people. My sincerest gratitude to my daughter Shenna and son-in-law Reece who asked me to write this book, coming up with some of the characters and content, to take my focus off my illness and redirect it to something we are all passionate about: diverse and inclusive books.

My daughter Raia-Sunshine, my handbag, for her creative ideas, 'child friendly' word checking and patience. My daughter Mari for her long-distance phone consultations. Shay and Rayne, my beautiful grandsons, for their encouragement, invitations to watch them play football for research, for checking the football skills in the book were described accurately and for their belief in what I was writing, renaming me their 'football gran.'

My dear friend Joanne Meekes for her constant support and advice and spreadsheets and the rest!

Saranna Maynard a real-life football mum for reading and re-reading my manuscript for authenticity.

To Abiola and Helen for their advice and patience.

To all the staff at St Bartholomew's Hospital London, who saved my life so I could write this book.

And finally, to all the children I've ever taught, a bit of each of you is somewhere in the characters.

Definition of a Baller Boy:

A player who is exceptional at football,
passionate about the game
and can execute skills to perfection.

SPEED: 98
TACKLE: 89
POWER: 93

COACH

COACH JOE

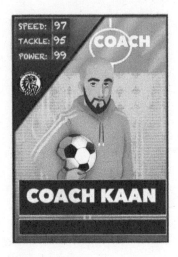

SPEED: 97
TACKLE: 95
POWER: 99

COACH

COACH KAAN

SPEED: 97
TACKLE: 95
POWER: 99

COACH

COACH REECE

JAMIE

SPEED: 75
TACKLE: 68 LEFT WINGER
POWER: 87

BLESSING

SPEED: 35
TACKLE: 48 DEFENDER
POWER: 91

SPEED: 67
TACKLE: 65 Goalkeeper
POWER: 82

Maxwell

FRANKIE

SPEED: 76
TACKLE: 75 **Midfield**
POWER: 87

SPEED: 58
TACKLE: 73
POWER: 82

CENTRE MID

HASSAN

SHAY

SPEED: 75
TACKLE: 68 **STRIKER**
POWER: 87

4

TANDEEP

SPEED: 43
TACKLE: 54
POWER: 46
RIGHT WINGER

SPEED: 79
TACKLE: 85
POWER: 62
Defender

TROY

SPEED: 76
TACKLE: 45
POWER: 72

OSCAR
MIDFIELDER

CHAPTER 1
Football Crazy

"Dad! Dad!" screeched Shay as he jumped on his parent's bed to shake his dad awake. "Get up! It's time to get ready."

Danny looked at his eldest son through sleepy eyes. Shay was dressed in his favourite football kit that had the number ten on the back. Long red football socks were pulled up to his knees with his shin pads tucked inside. On his feet were the well-used, orange and lime-green football boots that just needed the laces to be tied.

This was Danny's job. He always liked to make sure they were done up nice and tight.

Shay's Afro hair had been combed out into the usual

high top. His teeth had been brushed and he smelt of his dad's new aftershave. He had splashed a little on for luck and was hoping his dad wouldn't notice.

Finally, across his chest hung the black and white bag he took everywhere with him. Shay had prepared his clothes and packed his bag the night before.

For once, Shay had gone to bed on time, without using a single excuse to stay up later than his eight o'clock bedtime. He'd usually try, "Can I have some water?" or "I haven't finished my homework" (even though he had). But his favourite was, "Now that I'm eight and three quarters can I stay up a bit later?"

His mum and dad looked at each other in surprise when he'd put away his football cards and simply declared, "Goodnight, I'm going to bed."

Danny stifled a smile, then rolled over in his bed and looked at the bright red numbers on the LED clock. It read 6:22am.

"It's not time yet, Cheeky Chops, and don't think I can't smell it. You're way too young to be wearing my aftershave," Dad whispered.

"Shhh, keep your voice down," Shay's mum, Joanne hissed. "I don't want you to wake your brother up."

As soon as the words left Joanne's lips, four-year-old Rayne, with his freshly twisted hair dangling in front of his eyes, waddled into the room. He was wearing his Paw Patrol pyjamas. He rubbed his eyes and then yawned.

"Can I have breakfast please?" he asked.

This was quickly followed by a loud rumbling noise, which seemed to come from the depths of Rayne's pyjama bottoms.

"Oh, Rayne!" cried Joanne as she pulled the pillow over her head in anticipation of what would come next.

Danny and Shay quickly pinched their noses.

"Oops!" said Rayne, wiggling his bottom.

Everyone laughed except for Joanne who was still buried under her pillow with only the red of her night-time hair scarf showing.

*

Two doors down the street, Shay's best friend Frankie was also wide awake.

Shay and Frankie had been best friends since they'd met at Parkfield Nursery in North London. They'd gone on to Parkfield Primary School and found themselves sitting together in their first class. Now aged eight and about to begin Year Four, they were still the best of friends.

Frankie tiptoed into his parents' bedroom, not wanting to wake up his new baby brother.

As Frankie peeped into the room, his mum Tina smiled, she was sitting up in bed feeding the baby.

Katie, his younger sister, was beside their mum in her favourite, pink-and-white, spotty, Minnie Mouse pyjamas. She was holding her pink blankie and sucking her thumb.

"Good morning, Frankie. How are you feeling about today?" Tina asked.

Frankie shrugged his shoulders and turned to leave the room.

"Frankie, wait love. You'll be fine and I'm sure the

extra training you've been doing with Dad and Uncle Danny will have helped," Tina said softly.

Frankie looked at his mum thoughtfully and was about to say something when he was interrupted by his sister Katie yawning loudly.

"Don't I get a kiss?" Tina asked.

Frankie walked over to the bed and gave his mum a kiss on the cheek. He then looked at his baby brother and smiled. He was a proud big brother and was hoping that they would name him Sanchez after his favourite football player.

As he tried to leave the room again, his little sister Katie squealed, "Me too! Where's my kiss?"

Frankie sighed and walked to the side of the bed where she was sitting.

As Katie threw her arms around his neck and kissed him on his nose, her blankie fell to the floor. Frankie quickly, but gently, undid her arms and picked it up.

"Here you go," he said handing it back to her. The last thing he needed today was Katie having one of her tantrums.

As Frankie tried to leave for the third time, Katie said, "What about the baby? You've got to kiss the baby or it won't be fair!"

Frankie looked at his mum who was already holding the baby up for him to kiss.

As he walked back over his eyes grew wider.

"Please Mum, can we call him Sanchez? That name would be perfect for him!"

Frankie planted a kiss on his brother's forehead. As Tina chuckled, the baby began to fuss. Unbuttoning her gown, she placed the baby against her chest and began to feed. He quickly settled.

"You're such a good boy Frankie and a great big brother," Tina said softly. "His name will come to us. Just as yours and Katie's did."

"Okay. . . but just let it be Sanchez."

As Frankie stood stroking his baby brother's cheek, Tina

admired all three of her children. Frankie and Katie had taken after her with their caramel-coloured skin and tight, kinky, dark hair, but so far, the baby looked more like her husband Colin with fair skin and straighter blonde hair.

As Frankie stood gazing at the baby, he heard a noise in the kitchen. He knew it would be his dad getting home from work. Excited by his arrival, Frankie raced down the stairs to see if his dad had any more advice that would help him.

Today was going to be a big day for Shay and Frankie, and no doubt for lots of other boys that lived in their local area.

Just before school had broken up for the summer holiday, they had found out about the football trials and Shay and Frankie were going to try out.

CHAPTER 2

School's Out For Summer

Four weeks before the football trials, Shay sat tapping his foot impatiently in his classroom. His bag was slung over his shoulder and staring at the clock didn't seem to be making the time move any faster!

Frankie, sat next to Shay, was squinting at the clock. He knew it was nearly home time, but the numbers on the clock looked blurry.

A loud knock at the classroom door made the whole class jump.

A girl from Year Six walked in with a pile of letters for the teacher. Shay's foot stopped its tapping as the teacher passed smaller piles to the front of each row and requested each child hand the letters along.

Moments later, the bell rang, signalling the start of the long-awaited summer break. Most of the children, Shay and Frankie included, just stuffed the letters into their book bag without even giving them a second look, before darting out the door.

Shay spotted his mum standing with Frankie's mum on the playground. Rayne and Katie were on their scooters and Shay was excited to see their mums had brought their scooters along too. He ran over with Frankie on his heels.

The boys eagerly jumped on their scooters. Shay handed over his school bag and was already off! Frankie was about to follow him but his mum held him back.

"How was your last day in Year Three?" Tina asked, but Frankie was too busy looking at how far ahead of him Shay had gone. "Did you get any letters about next term, love?"

Bouncing on the balls of his feet, he shrugged his shoulders in response.

Tina rolled her eyes. "Go on then. I'm sure you'll catch him up."

"Thanks Mum," Frankie said as he sped off.

Joanne, however, had already rifled through Shay's bag, looking for newsletters and reports from school.

She had found the sticky, crumpled-up leaflet amongst two or three other letters. After straightening it out, she let out a little snort.

"No doubt if you'd read this, it would be in a better state!" she called out to Shay, now too far ahead to hear.

Tina peeked over her shoulder and agreed with a soft laugh. "Oh, the dynamic duo will definitely be interested in that!"

They walked out of the school towards home. As they turned onto their road, Rayne suddenly stopped his scooter.

"Mummy, can we go to the park first. Just for five minutes, please?"

Katie's eyes lit up at the mention of the word 'park' and as if by magic, the 'dynamic duo' Shay and Frankie stopped their scooters and turned around to listen for the answer.

The mums looked at each other and laughed, then gestured their children towards the park, as they tried to keep up behind them.

Shrieks of laughter filled the play area. It was full of school children already enjoying the freedom of the summer holiday.

"Oi! Pass us the ball," a boy yelled as a football whizzed towards Frankie.

Frankie caught the ball on his chest and the boys ran off to join the football game without a second thought, whilst Rayne and Katie headed for the swings.

Joanne collected the scooters the boys had dumped on the floor. Tina walked ahead, trying to catch up with Katie and Rayne.

Joanne glanced over at the boys and noticed that they were in a huddle with their classmates.

"I wonder what's going on over there?" she murmured to herself.

Suddenly, Shay and Frankie came racing back, eyes wide with excitement, almost tripping over their own feet.

"Mum, can I have my bag please?" Shay asked reaching for it before she had a chance to respond.

Frankie did the same and fished out the leaflet that they hadn't bothered to look at earlier.

"Hassan was telling the truth!" Frankie said with his eyes wide. "He said his team are looking for new players."

"Can we go?" Shay asked.

"Can we try?" Frankie said. "It says Coach Reece will be there!"

The two mums slyly looked at each other.

"What's all this about?" asked Joanne, pretending not to know.

"FOOTBALL TRIALS!" shouted Shay and Frankie in unison.

Joanne and Tina laughed.

"We know! We're just messing with you!" Tina said. "And yes of course you can both try out."

"We wouldn't let you miss it," Joanne said.

"Yes!" Shay shouted, punching the air. "And I can

ask Dad to bring us to the park more during the holidays to do some extra training!" He held out his hand and Frankie high-fived him.

CHAPTER 3

We Can Do This!

"Dad, Frankie and his mum are here. Come on let's go. I don't want to be late!" Shay shouted up the stairs before he raced to open the front door.

"Morning Shay," Tina said, walking into the house with Frankie behind her.

"Morning love," Joanne said, greeting Tina with a hug.

"Thanks for taking Frankie." Tina looked gratefully at her friend.

"No need for thanks. When he makes it as a professional baller, he can give me a cut of his first million!" said Joanne.

Tina laughed. "Oh, he will! Right, better get home

so Colin can get some sleep. He's just got back from his night-shift and I've left him with the baby. Good luck boys."

Frankie ran up to her for one last hug. Tina kissed him on the forehead and whispered in his ear, "You'll be amazing."

She closed the door gently on her way out.

"Right everyone, let's go," said Danny, zipping up Rayne's jacket.

"It's about time," said a frustrated Shay with his arms crossed over his chest.

"Shay, have you got your bag?" Joanne asked.

"Yes, look, I'm wearing it, and yes, I've got everything in it. I checked."

He unzipped his bag so his mum could peer inside.

"Good boy. Right then, let's go."

When everyone was loaded into the car, Joanne went around to check Shay and Frankie had put their seat belts on properly, before strapping Rayne into his booster seat.

"Mummy, you forgot something," giggled Rayne.

"I have. . . what?"

Rayne pointed to her head. "Your scarf that you wear to bed. You've still got it on."

Joanne put her hand up to her head and pulled it off. She looked at Danny and the three boys who were all laughing.

Joanne rolled her eyes. "Someone could have mentioned it," she said before joining in with the laughter.

"Right boys, how are you both feeling?" asked Danny looking through the rear-view mirror.

Shay and Frankie, who were both dressed in their favourite football kits, fell silent. They nervously looked at each other and neither of them replied.

"Just think about all the training and practice you've been doing to prepare for this," said Danny. "Your fitness has improved; your shooting is better. Shay, your penalty shots are great and Frankie your pace is phenomenal! Just go out there today and give it your best."

It was a short distance to Marshals Playing Fields but the roads were really busy. Traffic in North London on a Saturday was always bad. As they sat quietly waiting for the traffic to get moving, Joanne turned around in her seat to talk to the boys.

"You boys have been at the park with Dad more times than I can remember, practicing your drills and skills, always coming back tired and excited. Come on, you're ready for this!" Joanne frowned when neither of the boys said anything.

"Shay, this morning you said you were ready. What's changed?" asked Danny.

"Well, nothing Dad. I think I'm ready," Shay replied.

"Son, you were born ready and so were you Frankie, just give it—"

"Yes Dad, they know—give it their best shot," interrupted Rayne.

Everyone laughed and Rayne puffed out his chest, proud that he was able to lighten the mood.

Shay and Frankie glanced over at each other and smiled a secret smile that meant 'let's do this.'

With Rayne sitting between them in his booster seat, they stretched their hands across him to fist-bump each other. They were ready.

As Danny pulled into the car park at Marshals Playing Fields, Shay pressed his face against the window. The place was packed. Danny stopped the car to look around for a space to park.

"Dad!" Shay yelled. "There's a space behind you. . . quickly squeeze in."

"Good eye, Shay," Danny said as he reversed the car.

"Wow! I wasn't expecting to see so many people here," Shay said.

"Neither was I," Frankie said, budging Shay up so he could have a better view.

"Come on boys, let's get you registered," Danny said as he stepped out the car and stretched his arms into the air. He was ready and so were the boys!

CHAPTER 4

The Trials

Danny led the boys to the registration table whilst Joanne went with Rayne to chat with another mum by the pitch.

"So, who have we got here then?" asked the man sitting behind the desk. He was dressed in a red and black football top with an AC United badge.

"I'm Shay and this is my best friend Frankie," Shay said. He looked from left to right. "Where's Coach Reece? Is he here?"

Coach Reece had been a great player when he was younger and everyone had nicknamed him Baller Boy. Now he was one of the founders and head coach at AC United. He coached one of the older teams but he was always on the lookout for exceptional footballers. The future Ballers Boys.

The man laughed. "Yes, he's around somewhere."

Danny handed him the registration forms and the man had a quick look at them.

"Okay, I see that you're both eight. I'd like you to both go over there to that nice young man called Coach Joe. He's the one wearing the yellow bib and singing to himself. Tell him Pete, that's me, sent you over and listen to his instructions while I speak to your dad. Is that okay?"

Pete was a good man to know. He was the club secretary and in charge of all the paperwork. After every trial the coaches would sit down with Pete to discuss who would receive the good news about getting a place on the team via email or a telephone call.

But first, the boys had to impress! They nodded at Pete and ran in the direction of Coach Joe.

The white-lined pitches had been freshly marked out on the green grass and football nets were in position at each end. A man with a large megaphone was shouting out information. He told the parents they were welcome to stay and watch, but they were not allowed to cross the lines onto the pitches.

"Anyone under nine, come over here please!" Coach Joe shouted.

Wow, there must be at least five hundred boys here, Shay thought.

In fact, it was closer to two hundred boys trying out for all the age groups, with at least thirty trying out for the under-nines team, including returning players.

Coach Joe gestured for them to sit down, so Shay and Frankie sat down on the grass with their legs outstretched.

"Welcome to the AC United trials. My name is Coach Joe and this is Coach Kaan."

Coach Kaan took his hand out of his pocket to wave at the boys. He had a large brown beard and looked younger than the other coaches. He wore a baseball cap low that hid a lot of his face.

"We're really pleased that you'd like to play for our club and we look forward to some new faces joining us. All we ask of you is to try your best. You're here to have fun, meet new people and show us your skills. If you don't make the team today, don't worry, you're still welcome to come along and train with us in our development squad to improve your skills," Coach Joe explained.

Everyone sat quietly listening to what Coach Joe was saying, except for one boy who kept fidgeting and making noises. Shay also noticed another boy who was sitting by himself. He wore a scarf on his head that was tied around a bun. He kept his eyes to the ground.

Shay glanced over at Hassan, one of his classmates. It was alright for him. He was already on the team.

In fact, quite a few of the boys trying out today were already on the team.

"We'll be looking at your dribbling skills today. We need to see you boys have possession of the ball and keep control as you move around the field, or towards the opposing team. Also, try to use small taps between each foot." Coach Joe moved his feet to demonstrate the actions as he explained what he wanted to see from the boys. "When you get some space see if you can add some pace. Any questions?" He looked around at the players.

No one said anything.

"As you all know, football is a team sport, so we're expecting to see you working together by passing the ball. If you, or someone on your team, is under attack, you'll have to pass the ball to keep possession. We'll be looking out for speed and control. Any questions at this stage?"

"Do we need to show you *all* the different passes?" asked one of the boys.

"You'll need to use whichever one works best for you," replied Coach Joe. "Who thinks they can tell me some passes you might use?"

Shay put his hand up. Coach Joe pointed at him.

"You could do a side foot pass, an outside flick or even a back-heel pass to trick your opponent."

"Good job! Using all parts of your foot is vital in

handling the ball. That's what makes an outstanding dribbler and I'm hoping to see you use them." Coach Joe clapped his hands together and almost sang the words, "Right, let's get started."

The boys stood up to start the warm-up: a jog around the inside of their pitch, stretches, then different drills.

Shay loved the drills. He was great at taking penalties and they nearly always went in. He also enjoyed one-touch passing and was usually accurate with where he wanted the ball to end up, but dribbling was his absolute favourite. He especially loved to dribble past two or three of his opponents.

Today was no different for Shay and everything was going to plan. He knew the coaches would be watching. He wanted to impress them and stand out. Shay noticed that the fidgety boy had calmed down now and was really focused. Shay also noticed he was good—really good.

In the distance, Shay spotted a familiar figure walking towards the under-nines. He'd seen him before in the local newspapers and on the television. The man wasn't as tall as Coach Joe. He was stocky with a shaved head. Immediately Shay began to smile. The trademark red jacket and black tracksuit bottoms confirmed it. Shay knew it was him. It was definitely Coach Reece.

Now that Shay had seen Coach Reece he felt even more inspired to try his absolute best. He could see Coach Reece speaking to Coach Joe and several other coaches, as they watched the players, but they were too far away for anyone to hear what they were saying. Shay prayed that they were saying good things about him and Frankie.

Shay watched two other boys who were already on the team and it was obvious why. The bigger boy with the low cut Afro was good at intercepting the ball and wasn't afraid to go in for the tackle. The shorter boy with the big Afro was a great goalkeeper. He even saved some of the shots from the penalty line. He dived a full stretch across the mouth of the goal and deflected the ball with the tip of his gloves and that wasn't easy. Shay knew that must have impressed the coaches.

While Shay went to the back of the line, waiting for his turn to dribble again, he could see Frankie and Hassan running against each other. They had to keep the ball under control and dribble it in and out of the cones.

Hassan was really competitive. Shay knew he wouldn't like it if Frankie outran him. At school, Hassan was known for his super tantrums. If he didn't win a race, or his team didn't win a game, he would walk off, sulk and not speak to anyone. He'd been known to whack the ball across the playground. Once he'd kicked the ball so hard it flew over the fence and landed on top of someone's car. He'd been in so much trouble with their teacher.

Frankie looked good, he had great control of the ball and was faster than Hassan. Shay was pleased for him but worried about Hassan's reaction.

Hassan looked upset and kicked the grass, but before he could do anything else, Shay noticed Coach Kaan shout something over to Hassan in Turkish. Hassan stopped kicking and walked off in a huff.

Next, Frankie was called by Coach Reece to have a turn at Cone Kick Down, which is played with two players against each other. Instead of having a goal to shoot at, Coach Reece set up five cones along each goal line. He looked around and pointed in Shay's direction, signalling him over. Shay looked around to see who Coach Reece was pointing at, then realised it was him.

"Me?" Shay questioned.

"Yes you, over here. You two are going against each other."

Shay walked over and stood opposite Frankie.

CHAPTER 5
Every Boy For Himself

Shay knew that Frankie would be feeling nervous. Whenever it came to penalty shots, Frankie rarely ever hit the target. Shay just hoped nerves wouldn't get the better of his best friend. Although he wanted Frankie to do well, he also knew that *he* had to do his best, so he tried to put Frankie out of his mind and focus.

Frankie and Shay were given a ball each and sent to stand back to back in the middle of the pitch facing their own goal line.

"When I blow the whistle, you have one minute to see how many cones you can hit by shooting your ball from the penalty line. Each time you kick your ball, you need to retrieve it and come back to the centre and start again."

Frankie stood in the centre and tried to focus on the cones. He could see their outline but they were blurred. He used the back of his hand to wipe his eyes, to see if that would help him refocus, but no change.

It must be nerves, he thought.

"I'm looking for speed and accuracy!" Coach Reece shouted. He glanced at his stopwatch, then when he was ready, he blew the whistle.

Frankie took his first shot and missed. He had no time to think about how Shay was doing, he had to retrieve his ball and keep going.

Frankie attempted six more shots. By the time Coach Reece blew the whistle Frankie was really upset. He knew he hadn't done well. He had managed to hit one cone. Frankie dropped his head and punched his hand into his fist. He was disappointed with himself. It didn't help that Shay had hit four out of five cones.

Shay was delighted with his performance and smiled from ear to ear. All the practice he had put in with his dad had paid off. As he turned around to look at Frankie, he could see the disappointment on his face.

"Don't worry, Frankie, you've still got time to show your other skills," Shay said, putting an arm around him.

Joanne nodded. "But if you start to feel like you need a break from running tell the coach."

"Okay Mum," Shay said even though he had no intention of doing so. He wanted to be on the team and nothing was going to stop him.

Shay had had asthma for as long as he could remember, and it had never stopped him from doing anything. In fact, the doctors had said sport was good for his type of asthma; it improved how well his lungs worked, so he would have more stamina and get less breathless.

Now that he was older, Mum and Dad had taught him to always carry his bag with the inhaler for his asthma and EpiPen for his nut allergy, after having a serious allergic reaction at a birthday party last year.

All the boys were sitting down having a quick drink, including the quiet boy with the headscarf who again sat away from everyone else. They eagerly listened to Coach Joe explain what was going to happen next. All except one; the fidgety boy. He was off again, kicking a stone around and doing cartwheels.

"Boys, if anyone fancies themselves as a goalie, you're up next. You'll be in goal for some penalty shots, then you'll be in goal for the five-a-side later on. Any questions?" The boys looked around at each other but no one said anything.

"Jamie? Jamie sweetheart," a red-haired lady with

eckles called to the fidgety boy. "Come here now. You
eed to drink some water and listen to your coach."

Every now and again, Coach Joe would look up
at Jamie but left him alone. Some of the boys looked
at each other, then at Jamie, then at Coach Joe. They
couldn't understand why he wasn't being told off or
made to listen.

Coach Reece and Coach Kaan walked back to where
the boys were sitting. They stood looking and talking
quietly to each other before signalling to get Coach
Joe's attention.

Everyone sat waiting, wondering what the next part
of the trial would be.

CHAPTER 6

Run Like The Wind

"Joe, can you get the boys into groups of ten for the sprints? And then send them over to the line, where I'll be waiting. Kaan will be at the other end."

Coach Reece and Coach Kaan went to their ends of the pitch, whilst Coach Joe turned to the boys.

"I'll put you into groups and you'll do a few runs. We need to see your stamina and speed, so I want you to run like the wind." Coach Joe smiled as he talked.

Frankie was in the first group of boys. As soon as Coach Reece shouted, "Go!" Frankie was off in front of all the boys and stayed in pole position for the entire race. Frankie smiled from ear to ear.

Shay was in the next group that included the quiet

but very quick boy. Shay did his best and finished third. Although he was a little disappointed with his performance, he was pleased he hadn't come last. The quiet boy came in first place.

The boys ran several races each before the coaches asked some of them to sit out and take a break.

As the final group of ten, which included Shay, Frankie and Hassan, were called to the line by Coach Reece, Joanne watched her son coughing as he walked to the line and wondered if he might need his inhaler again.

"Ready boys? Go!" yelled Coach Reece.

Ten pairs of legs flew down the pitch towards Coach Joe and Coach Kaan. Frankie was a little bit faster and he narrowly beat Hassan. Shay was sixth and the quiet boy came fifth.

"Well done boys. Get yourselves a drink and take five minutes," said Coach Kaan. He walked towards Coach Reece who was holding a clipboard and papers.

As the other parents clapped and called out encouraging words to their sons, as they slowly made their way back over to the others, Danny and Joanne called Shay over to check on him and give him his inhaler.

"Right guys, it's time for some five-minute five-a-side," Coach Joe said. "Jamie, over here please and join the boys on this team."

Jamie came over at once, wiping his long, red, tangled hair from his face and mouth. He hopped from one foot to the other, and twisted his hands so rapidly he almost fell over from all the movement. Shay noticed one of the other players, who was wearing a top with the name 'Troy' on the back, snigger at the fidgety boy.

The five-aside matches started with four players and a goalkeeper on each team. Most of the dads and some of the mums were calling out instructions to their children.

"Good shot, Oscar!" called a mum holding a baby.

"Go on Tandeep! Down the middle!" shouted one dad.

"Control it and keep it close to you!" shouted another.

"That's it, Jamie love, tackle!" screamed the lady with red hair and freckles.

Shay could hear his dad shouting, "Well done, Shay! Beautiful passing! Get in there Frankie. Don't worry lad, keep going."

Coach Reece mixed the teams up again and again, with each boy eventually playing four different matches. Finally, the whistles blew across the pitches. Shay and Frankie were exhausted!

"Well done everyone and thanks for coming," said Coach Joe. "You should all feel very proud of yourselves for turning up today and having a go. We'll be in touch with your parents in a day or two!"

And that was it. The football trials were over.

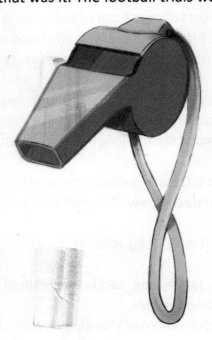

CHAPTER 1

The Big Wait

On the way home Shay and Frankie talked and talked about nothing else but the football trials. They talked about what they thought they'd done well, what they weren't happy with, which other boys were good, if Coach Reece had spotted them, and about the fidgety boy.

As Danny parked the car outside his house, Shay and Frankie carried on their conversation. Joanne took Rayne inside so she could start their dinner—a family favourite of rice and peas with jerk chicken.

"Let's pop into Frankie's so I can update his mum and dad on how it went today," suggested Danny. Their dads had been friends for years. They had grown up in the same area and attended the same secondary school. Whenever they got together, they liked to talk about "the good old days."

Frankie pressed his doorbell. It was one of those bells that sang a long tune.

"Frankie, your doorbell is so annoying," said Shay covering his ears.

"Yeah, I know." Frankie laughed, pressing it again, and Shay groaned.

Tina peered through the living room curtain before coming to answer the front door.

"Hi guys, how did it go?" she asked, ruffling Frankie's hair and loosening one of his plaits from his red hair band. She ushered everyone in. "Where's Joanne?"

"She went straight in to get dinner sorted. We're all starving! Is Colin about? I wanted to tell you both how Frankie got on today," Danny said.

"He came home late. Let me see if he's still sleeping," said Tina. There was a creak on the stairs. "Oh, there he is."

Colin was a tall man and he seemed to shrink every room he was in. He was gently carrying the baby as he walked down the stairs. They both looked as though they'd just woken up.

"Danny, my man, how's things?" Colin handed the baby to Tina and shook Danny's hand.

"Yeah good and you? Rescue any cats from trees last night?"

"Very funny." Colin rolled his eyes, but he was smiling. "That joke's getting stale now."

Frankie's dad was a fire fighter and was very proud of his job. He'd been in the fire service since he left school. He loved his work but he just wished he had more time to spend with Tina and the family. Working shifts often meant he was at work when Frankie came in after school or on important days like this, when he wanted to be the one to take his son to football trials. Colin felt really grateful to have a good friend like Danny, even if he did tell silly jokes.

"So, how did my boy get on at the big trial? Thanks for taking him," said Colin, running his hands through his short, blonde, cropped hair. He rubbed his bright blue eyes, trying to fully wake himself up.

"He did us all proud and gave it his best shot. You know Frankie. He's fast and outran all of the other boys on the pitch!"

"That's Frankie alright!" Colin said proudly. "How was Shay?"

"Really good. All we have to do now is wait! AC United said they'd be in touch with everyone in a day or so."

Frankie and Shay looked at each other. They would just have to keep their fingers crossed that they both made the team.

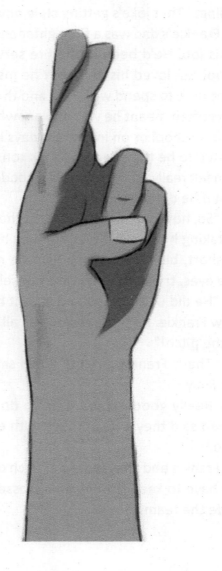

CHAPTER 8

Are We In?

Monday afternoon arrived. Frankie found himself staring out of the window, waiting for his dad to get home, to find out if he'd heard anything about the trials. Every time a car pulled up outside, he'd race to the window to see if it was him. So far, he'd had no luck.

Shay was at the park playing football with his dad and younger brother Rayne when his dad's mobile rang.

"Hello? Yes, this is Shay's dad. Oh, hello Coach Joe."

Shay froze on the spot. He looked up at his dad and held his breath.

It had been quite a difficult job for the coaches at AC United, but they'd finally selected their teams. Giving good news was easy, but all the coaches found it difficult to tell the families that their sons hadn't made the team.

The coaches had promised that all the families would be contacted and told if their child had made it into the club—either the main team or the development squad.

In total there would be twenty boys in the under-nines group. Ten would be part of the main team. There would be seven players and three reserves. The other ten would be in the development squad who would train and improve their skills and then hopefully get a chance to play in the main team in the future.

The wait was finally over for Shay and his family. He waited nervously as his dad finished the conversation. Shay's dad hung up the phone and broke into a huge smile.

"You got in!"

"Yesssss!" Shay said punching the air.

When they got home, Shay ran around the living room with his sweater over his face, screaming at the top of his voice. His little brother Rayne joined in and they began to do a victory dance. Shay got so hot from all the celebrating he took his jumper off.

Dad took a selfie of them on his phone, adding the caption 'Our boy made the team!' and sent it to Joanne at work, who cheered out loud when she saw it. The whole family was delighted for him.

Shay thought about his best friend and wondered if Frankie had found out yet.

"Mum, can I go online to see if Frankie's on his computer?"

"Okay, but just for a minute."

Shay ran into the living room and switched on his computer. He could see that Frankie was online and tried to speak to him, but Frankie didn't answer.

CHAPTER 9

Thanks, But No Thanks!

When Coach Reece had called Colin that afternoon, it wasn't the news that Frankie had hoped for. Colin and Tina had both felt so disappointed for their son.

"Come here, son." Colin put his arms around him, hugging him close. "Listen to me, you're a good player and you will get better. The coaches have obviously seen something in you, which is why they've asked you to join the development squad. They don't just let anyone in. You must have some special skills and I know that you do. Don't worry, just keeping working hard."

Frankie shook his head, then the tears came. "But Dad, I did try hard. I really did."

"Yes, I know you did son. I know you're a good

player. Maybe it was just that some of the other players shined a bit more on the day. Look, once you start training, you'll definitely improve and as long as you keep giving it your all, they're bound to notice you."

As Frankie sobbed into his dad's arms, Colin carefully tucked some of the plaits that had fallen out of his son's hairband back into place. He gently wiped his tears away and kissed him on the top of his head.

Even after the chat with his dad, Frankie didn't feel any better. He didn't want to be on the development squad. That wasn't what he'd tried out for.

That's it! I'm not going to accept the place, he thought.

For a moment he wondered about Shay and thought he should call him back. But he didn't want to tell anyone that he hadn't made the team. He fell on to his bed, switched on his TV, but didn't watch it, instead he buried his head into his pillow and sobbed quietly.

Later that evening, just before bed, Shay tried again to talk to his friend on the computer and this time Frankie answered.

"Frankie! I made the team! I'm so happy. This is our dream come true. The best day of our life so far! Coach rang my dad and we did a dance to celebrate, even my dad joined in." Shay laughed but he abruptly stopped when he realised Frankie wasn't laughing with him. "Frankie, are you there? Frankie?"

Shay could hear him breathing but just not saying anything.

"You alright mate?" Shay asked. "You did make the team as well, didn't you?"

Frankie could barely bring himself to answer, he took a few deep slow breaths before answering. "No. I only made the development squad."

"The development squad? What! Are you joking?"

Frankie didn't answer and it took Shay a moment to realise it wasn't a joke.

"Oh, erm. . . don't worry Frankie, that's still good! You just need to work on passing. I can help if you like?"

"No need," Frankie replied. "I've decided not to take the place. I think my football days are well and truly over."

"But Frankie, you can't quit! You're really good," protested Shay.

"Well, if I'm that good, why didn't I get picked then? Why did they just pick *you*?" asked Frankie, almost shouting at his friend, and then the tears came again. "Shay, I've got to go and I'm sorry. Well done for making the team. See you later."

The computer screen went black. Shay sighed and shut down his computer. He didn't know how to feel. Frankie had been his best friend for as long as he could remember. They went to school together, always played football together and had planned to join AC United together. They were more than friends; they were like brothers. Now everything would change. They wouldn't be able to play together in matches.

Will I even see him at training? Will we still be best friends? Shay shook his head. He was being silly! They were solid, and team or no team they would be as close as ever.

CHAPTER 10

Welcome To AC United

All the boys selected for the main team and the development squad were asked to come to Marshals Playing Field on Saturday morning at midday.

The boys were told to wear their training kit, football boots, shin pads, gloves (if they'd tried out as a goalkeeper) and to bring a bottle of water. They were also told to be on time.

Frankie's mum checked her phone for the weather forecast: cloudy with a chance of rain. It was the first day of football training and she would be taking Frankie, Katie and the baby.

Tina was so happy when Frankie changed his mind and said he would accept a place on the development squad. To make him smile, she decided to give his baby brother, newly named Thomas, the middle name Sanchez, which had cheered Frankie up.

Frankie got dressed in his red and white AC uniform. His dad had bought him a new pair of football boots and shin pads to go with the new kit.

Frankie looked in the mirror and said to his reflection, "I will make the team. Watch and see!"

"Come on Frankie. It's time to go!" Tina called, as she pulled on Katie's jacket. "You don't want to be late on the first day."

Marshals Playing Field wasn't as busy as it had been on the day of the trials. Shay was practically bouncing on his feet. He couldn't wait to get started.

He saw the fidgety boy, Jamie, arrive with his mum who today had bright pink hair.

"Mum, that's the boy I told you about. The one that can't keep still and doesn't listen." Shay pointed at Jamie.

Joanne, who was busy pulling out snacks and drinks from her bag, looked up and saw Jamie almost knock Katie off her scooter. Jamie paused for a moment, but then carried on running, full steam ahead.

Tina gasped and shook her head at Jamie's actions. As she bent down to see to her daughter, she noticed Joanne quickly walking towards them looking alarmed.

Coach Reece appeared ten minutes later and called the boys over to welcome them to AC United. Shay was delighted that Coach Reece was there.

"I'm pleased that you're all here on time and I must say, you look great in your training kits," Coach Reece said and Shay beamed. "We here at All Cultures United are proud of everyone that tried out for the team. I know some of you are in our development squad, but I want you to know that you're here because you have the potential to be in the main team."

Frankie sat listening carefully to Coach Reece's words and found himself firmly repeating to himself, under his breath, "I will make this team. I will, I will, I will."

Next, Pete went through the register and asked each boy to shout, 'here,' if they were present. All of the players answered except for Jamie who shook his head then proceeded to pick his nose. Tandeep, the very quiet boy, didn't answer but raised his hand instead. He spent most of the time looking down at his hands, avoiding everyone's eyes.

After the register, Pete went over to speak to the parents. "We're happy for you to go and leave the boys here with us, as long as you're back for the end of training to collect them on time. You're more than welcome to stay and watch, but please remember to let the coaches do the coaching."

"I'm going to stay for a while," Tina said to Joanne as they walked to the stands. "Then I'll take Katie and the baby over to the swings for a bit. I can take Rayne as well if you like?"

"I'll come with you," replied Joanne.

The two mums stayed with the other parents while the boys started their warm-up. Then the boys were split into two groups. Shay and Frankie weren't in the same group.

Coach Joe took the main team while Coach Kaan took the development squad. Coach Reece stood on the side lines watching.

The main team consisted of Shay, Hassan, Blessing, Troy, Oscar, Maxwell the goalkeeper, Tandeep and Jamie.

As the two groups parted Shay looked over at Frankie and gave him a big thumbs up. Frankie smiled back weakly, wishing he could stay with Shay in the main team.

CHAPTER 11

Settling In

Training started with what would become their usual routine. The warm-up was a few laps around the pitch, star jumps and knee kicks. This was followed by shoulder rolls, hip, knee and ankle rotations, butt kicks, dribbling and drills.

The coaches knew that a consistent routine was good. It helped the players to know what was coming and the coaches knew it was especially helpful for Jamie to have some structure. Jamie had ADHD, which meant that he was often impulsive, doing things without thinking it through first. He was hyperactive, which meant he was always on the go. Because of this, the other children called him 'fidgety boy.' Having an organised warm-up routine helped Jamie to stay focused, which meant he was less likely to become distracted and fidget.

The coaches threw in a few games designed to make the boys feel relaxed and help them to get to know each other, which in turn helped them to work together better. It also helped to prepare the boys for the harder training that was to follow and, of course, the matches.

At the end of the first session, Joanne and Tina arrived to take the boys home. The boys grabbed their bags and walked towards their mums, who noticed that Frankie was quiet and sulky, while Shay was excited and smiling.

"Frankie, come here son, you looked good out there today. How did it go?" asked Tina.

As Shay and Joanne looked on, Frankie shook his shoulders and almost pleaded, "Can we go home now please?"

"Training was brilliant! I really enjoyed it, did you?" asked Shay.

Frankie didn't answer, instead he pulled his mum's arm hoping to hurry her along so they could leave. He was still very disappointed at not making the team and didn't want to talk about it. He wanted them both on the team or both in the development squad. He really didn't want to believe that Shay was any better than he was.

*

Every week, the coaches put the under-nines through their paces and they got better and better. The coaches made a point of praising the players for both their individual and team development.

As time went on Frankie gradually began to enjoy being on the development squad. Every time the coaches praised him; he grew in confidence. He showed his commitment by attending training regularly. In fact, he had never missed a session and he always gave his best, just like his dad had told him to do.

He was getting noticed for being a good midfielder because he was one of the fittest and fastest players in the squad. He could cover the pitch quickly, getting the ball from one end to the other.

Frankie watched the game carefully and always knew where he needed to direct the ball and who to pass to. He only wished that he was better at long shots and passing the ball with accuracy, but he was working on it. His dad had been helping him practice at the park whenever he had time. Although the boys on the development squad were friendly enough, Frankie preferred to stick with Shay and the players on the main team.

Shay was also enjoying playing for AC United and was making a name for himself as a striker. He was fantastic at getting himself into the right positions to score goals and was brilliant at creating chances for the other players to score. He had become a popular member of the club and enjoyed the company of the team and the development squad, often laughing and joking with all of them. All in all, football training was going well for both boys.

"Hey everyone," Hassan shouted, as the boys began picking up their stuff ready to go home. "My dad's invited the whole team, their parents and the coaches to our restaurant for a celebration lunch next Saturday after training."

"We're all invited for free food?" asked Shay.

"Yeah, you can have anything you like," Hassan said proudly.

"Frankie, did you hear that? You love Turkish food!" Shay said.

"Oh, sorry, no, Frankie can't come. It's only for the players on the *main* team not the development squad."

"Oh. . . it's okay," Frankie said quietly before picking up his bag and walking off.

"Frankie, wait up!"

Shay caught up with his friend and tried to put his arm around his shoulder, but Frankie shrugged him off. Shay was surprised by Frankie's reaction, in fact he felt a bit hurt, after all it wasn't his fault that Hassan had said what he'd said. Shay didn't really know what to say to Frankie, so they both walked over to their families in silence.

"You alright boys? What's that face for Frankie?" asked Joanne.

"Nothing," Frankie mumbled.

Joanne glanced at Shay who shook his head.

Tina gently ruffled Frankie's head. "Let's go home love."

CHAPTER 12

The Lie

"Mum, Hassan said his family have invited everyone on the team for lunch at their restaurant on Saturday, can I go?" asked Shay almost breathless with excitement.

"Aww lovely, of course you can. What type of food is it?" enquired Joanne.

"His family have a Turkish restaurant. You know that big one on the high street?"

"Oh yeah, I know the one. You lucky boy, wish I was going. I'll go on their website and take a look at the menu to see what food you can have and check their allergen statement." Joanne took her phone out of her bag and began to Google the restaurant. "As long as you take your bag with your EpiPen in, and I give you some antihistamines, you should be fine. Oh, I'll speak to Hassan's parents as well."

"Thanks Mum, you're the best, and. . . he said our families are invited too."

Joanne looked at her son, raised her eyebrows and smirked at him. "Ha ha! You're so funny."

"I'm not joking! Hassan said all of our families are invited as well."

"Oh wow that's generous of them! Tina and Frankie are going to love this. They love Turkish food."

"Well, actually Mum, that's why Frankie was upset after training today. Hassan said it's only for the main team, so he can't come."

Joanne switched off the kettle and stopped making her coffee to give Shay her full attention.

"Ah, poor Frankie that must have been upsetting for him." Joanne studied Shay carefully. "How do you feel about him not coming?"

Shay thought about it for a moment then shrugged his shoulders. "I don't know. It will be a bit weird without him but I still want to go. I like the boys that I play with and I think it will be fun. Can I go on my computer?"

"Yeah sure. Maybe we can all go out together another time? That might cheer Frankie up, what do you think?"

Shay didn't answer, the lunch invite already a distant memory. As he threw himself down into his dad's gaming chair and logged on to his computer, he could see it was one of his teammates, Troy, inviting him into a game.

*

"Frankie, what's up love, you've been a bit quiet since we left training, has something happened?" Tina asked.

Frankie sighed. "It's that Hassan. He's trying to make Shay his best friend. He's really getting on my nerves."

"What happened? What did he do?"

"He invited Shay and everyone else on the team to his fancy restaurant and said it's only for the main team, so I can't go!" Frankie kicked his football bag and threw himself on to the sofa. He was well and truly fed up.

Tina sat down next to her son on the sofa. "Look, maybe it's something Hassan's family usually does. They invite the players to celebrate making the team? I'm sure they haven't arranged it to upset you or anyone else. It might not seem fair but don't take it personally."

Frankie thought about it for a moment. He knew his mum could be right but he still felt left out and upset.

He really wished he'd made the team then none of this would be happening. He wouldn't be feeling like he was losing his best friend.

Frankie went upstairs to his bedroom and noticed his computer flashing. As he got closer to the screen, he saw that it was Shay inviting him to join a game. Frankie smiled. Maybe their friendship was still okay.

*

The day of the lunch arrived and Hassan had asked everyone to arrive for midday. Hassan's dad had sectioned off an area of the restaurant just for the team's use. The restaurant was beautiful. It looked like it had just been renovated and there was an amazing waterfall at the front.

Inside the staff were smartly dressed, with big smiles on their faces, which made everyone feel welcome. They escorted the team to an area of the restaurant that had been specially decorated with football balloons. The parents were taken by the waiters to a separate area, where they ordered food for themselves and the boys.

Hassan saw Shay and waved him over to a seat next to him. He hurried over, high-fived him and sat down. As usual, Oscar arrived late with his two mums and baby sister, and rushed over to join the group.

As the conversations started getting louder, Shay noticed that most of the main team were there, but the whole development squad was also there. Everyone except Frankie.

"Err, Hassan, how come—"

But the food arrived and Shay got drowned out by the boys cheering.

The food was delicious with plenty of drinks. After the table was cleared, Troy shouted across the room, "Where's your bestie, Shay?"

Shay shrugged his shoulders and looked at Hassan who quickly turned away. Shay decided to try again to speak to him about it, but Hassan seemed to deliberately go into the office, where customers were not allowed.

As the families started to say goodbye, Hassan seemed to be taking his time saying goodbye to everyone. Joanne was eager to get home so Shay didn't have time to ask him about Frankie.

In the car, Shay didn't say a word.

"What's up Shay?" Joanne asked.

"Hassan said the development squad couldn't come, but they were all there, all except Frankie. Hassan didn't invite him on purpose."

"Oh, that's not nice. Maybe we should warn Frankie before he finds out. Let's stop there on the way home," she said.

"No Mum, I can't tell Frankie! It would only make things worse between us. Please, I don't want to be the one to tell him."

"Shay, are you sure? As his friend, it might be better coming from you," Joanne replied.

"No Mum, I'm sure, let's just go home."

Joanne looked at her son but didn't say another word.

CHAPTER 13

Frankie Learns The Truth

Several weeks later, with the evening air cooler than at the beginning of the season, Joanne took the boys to training. Rayne came too, dressed in his own football kit. He wanted to be just like his big brother Shay and was taking more interest in football. He had begun supporting his local team, and Danny had taken him and Shay to the club shop in Highbury, to buy his first real kit.

Joanne had become a real football mum. She did most of the training runs with Shay and Frankie and was impressed with how well their skills were developing.

"Thanks for bringing me, Aunty Joanne," Frankie said, as he climbed out of the car.

"You're welcome Frankie, and it's a pleasure to bring you. Shay, have you got your bag?" she called, watching Shay run over to his teammates.

"Don't worry Mum. I have it!" he called back over his shoulder without stopping.

"See you later," Frankie called, running along to catch Shay up.

Shay had gone ahead to join Hassan and the others without waiting for him, and this had made Frankie feel even more left out. Since Shay had made the team, he had become very popular with the players. He was invited around to their homes, had gone to the cinema, played in the park. Frankie was never invited.

By the time Frankie caught up with Shay and the others, they were already deep in conversation. None of them stopped chatting to even say hello to Frankie. With his head down, he walked on, deciding to leave Shay and the rest of them to it.

Frankie loved football so much, but he couldn't ignore that he was getting more and more distant with Shay, who spent so much time hanging out with the boys in the main team.

Frankie wished he could join in with their conversations and understand all their inside jokes.

Although he got on well with the boys from the development squad he couldn't help but feel like they were second best and in his eyes all of them were a substitute for Shay.

*

The coaches made the boys from both the main team and development squad train hard, they also made sure it was fun, and today was no different. Coach Joe was making up lyrics and singing out loud as usual. He fancied himself as a bit of a rapper and was always making up songs, which made the players laugh.

"You're out of tune Coach!" laughed Oscar as he ran past Coach Joe.

This made Coach Joe change his lyrics and rap even louder. "My mind's elevated, I might need to make some changes, cheeky kids might need to take a back seat. . ."

"No, no Coach, I'm just joking, I meant great tune." Oscar said.

The first half of training seemed to go quickly and it wasn't long before it was time for a break. After the break, the main team and development squad played a training match against each other.

Jamie's mum, Kathy, who today had light blue hair, brought the tray of water bottles over to the boys who had all flung themselves down on the grass.

"Help yourselves to water," she said, not taking her eyes off Jamie for a minute.

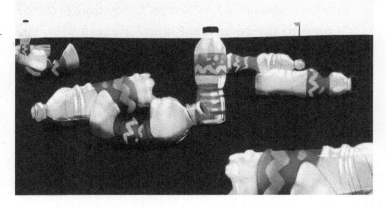

As the boys from the team and development squad sat on the grass together drinking their water, Blessing riffled through his bag, hoping he had something in there to munch on. He didn't.

"Guys, I'm starving, anyone got any snacks?" he asked hopefully.

"Yeah, I'm hungry as well. Hassan can we come back to your restaurant for some more food?" asked one of the players from the development squad.

"Yeah!" replied most of the boys.

"Frankie, you really missed out the other week. The food at Hassan's restaurant was so good. Why didn't you come?" asked Blessing.

"Yeah you were the only one that didn't join us," Oscar said. "Everyone was there."

As the boys turned to look at Frankie, he noticed both Shay and Hassan avoiding his eyes.

Frankie was stunned. *Why didn't Shay say anything?*

"Come to the restaurant later," Hassan said, still not looking at Frankie.

"Well, any snacks, anyone? Blessing needs food now, not at the end of the season," joked Oscar.

Everyone laughed and continued chatting amongst themselves. No-one seemed to notice how upset Frankie was.

Frankie turned his back and walked away, tears streaming down his face. He had been lied to. He didn't care about Hassan, but he couldn't believe that Shay, his best friend, would lie to him.

He began to run as fast as he could, past the coaches and parents, past Joanne who was waiting to take him home. He ran all the way to the car park and stopped by the car. He didn't want anyone to see him crying and at this moment he really hated Hassan and Shay.

"Mum, have you seen Frankie?" asked Shay running towards her.

"Yes, he just flew past me, running towards the car park I think. What's going on?" she yelled, as Shay flew past.

"He knows about the dinner," Shay replied, running in the direction of the car park to look for his friend.

As Shay approached the car park, he saw Frankie sitting in a heap on the ground next to the car, sobbing. Slowing down and walking towards him, he knew he had done the wrong thing by not telling him. He had wanted to spare Frankie's feelings, but the secret had made things worse.

"Frankie, are you alright? I'm sorry I didn't say anything to you about the dinner. Hassan lied to both of us when he said it was only for the main team. When I got there, I was shocked to see almost everyone there, then I didn't know how to tell you." Shay walked closer to Frankie and bent down on the floor beside him. "Frankie, I'm sorry, I was trying not to upset you."

Shay sat on the ground next to him. Frankie wiped his eyes.

"If you're *my* best friend, you shouldn't keep things from me. I would never keep anything like that from you."

"Yeah, I know, and I am really sorry. I won't do anything like that ever again, I promise. Come on man we're the dream team. Can we be cool? Please?" Shay pleaded to Frankie, making silly faces, trying to make him smile.

Joanne caught up with the boys, eyeing them cautiously. "Alright boys?" she asked hopefully.

Shay looked at Frankie, who gave him a weak smile.

"We're cool Mum," Shay said.

CHAPTER 14

The Mascot

Shay and Frankie were sitting with some of their teammates listening to Oscar telling jokes.

"You're so funny. If you weren't such a good player you could be our mascot," said Shay.

"You would be a good mascot," Frankie chimed in.

"What's a mascot?" Hassan frowned.

"Ahh, Hassan man, you're such a dummy." Troy laughed shaking his head. "Everyone knows what a mascot is!"

"Well, I don't," Hassan snapped, standing to his feet. "I wasn't asking you anyway!'

"Who are you shouting at?" Troy retorted, jumping up.

Shay quickly stood up so he was in-between Hassan and Troy. He pushed them back, away from each other.

"A mascot is meant to bring good luck to the club. They usually appear at games and they're kind of funny, they wear a costume and help to get the crowd excited," Shay explained.

"Oh, I know what you're talking about," Oscar said. "I've seen them at some of the matches on the TV. They're usually big and colourful and do silly things to make people laugh."

"I know what you mean now. I didn't know that's what they were called," Hassan said, sitting back down on the grass, but not before making a face at Troy.

Shay was relieved to see that both boys had calmed down.

"Hey, why don't we get one for the club? It would be great. It could come to all of our matches and be our biggest fan," Shay said.

"He could be red and black like our club colour and he could give out sweets," chipped in Troy.

"So, where do we get mascots from? And how much do they cost?" Hassan asked.

"Don't worry, we can figure it out together, with some special help." Shay winked.

Hassan frowned. "Special help from who?"

"Google!" said Shay.

The boys fell back on to the grass, laughing. Sitting quietly but not joining in, Tandeep had a big grin on his face. Shay laughed so hard he began to cough and wheeze.

"Do you need a puff on your inhaler?" Frankie asked, putting an arm around him.

"Yeah, thanks mate."

Frankie tossed him his bag and Shay pulled out his inhaler. He took in some deep breaths, giving a thumbs-up to Frankie.

"I have an idea!" Frankie said. "Why don't we pay for it ourselves?"

All at once the boys replied, "I don't have any money!"

"Why can't the club pay for it? We could ask the coaches?" suggested Troy.

"We could ask my dad. He's got lots of money," boasted Hassan.

"What would be the fun in that? We can think of some cool ways to earn money and how much better would it be having a mascot that we got ourselves, as a team?" Shay said.

"What things can we do to fundraise?" Frankie asked.

"My mum and her friends do sponsored swims to raise money for a charity that helped my grandma when she wasn't well." said Shay.

"Oh, I can't swim very well," said Troy.

"Neither can I," said Hassan.

"We don't have to swim. We could do a sponsored run and we can definitely all run," Oscar said, sprinting in a circle around the group of boys to make his point.

"What's wrong with your grandma?" asked Hassan.

"She has something wrong with her blood and it was making her really sick, it's a funny word. Leu. . . something, I can't remember."

"It's Leukaemia, isn't it?" Frankie said.

"Oh, yeah that's it," Shay said. "My grandma has Leukaemia. My mum and her friends raised loads of money and my grandma was really happy. We could raise loads of money to get a mascot!"

Not far from them, Jamie was dribbling a ball around. Shay noticed how fast and skilful he was; the ball never got away from him.

"Guys, look at Jamie. Look how fast he can run and his control of the ball! Let's ask him to help, actually, all the boys can help," suggested Shay.

"Sorry, not Jamie," Troy said frowning at Jamie. "He's weird and annoying."

"No, he's—" but Shay was cut off by Coach Joe's whistle.

"Come on boys! Up you get!"

They spent the rest of the session practicing

penalties and Shay was counting down the minutes until they could speak to Coach Reece about the mascot idea.

As soon as the whistle blew Shay, Frankie, Troy, Oscar and Hassan ran over to Coach Reece, with Tandeep slowly walking behind them.

"Everything okay boys?" Coach Reece asked, as he picked up the cones from the pitch.

"Coach we think it would be really cool if the club had a mascot," Shay said.

"Okay, tell me more," replied Coach Reece. He put down the cones he'd been collecting to give them his full attention.

"We think a mascot at our games would get everyone excited for the match. Plus, we want to work together to raise the money to buy the costume," Frankie explained.

"And who would be the mascot?" Coach Reece asked.

"We haven't thought about that bit yet. Oscar would be great but he's on the team. . . we want someone just as funny as Oscar," Shay said.

"And we're going to do a sponsored run," Oscar added.

"That sounds good boys. Mascots are usually an animal. Do you know what animal you'd like?"

"What about a bear or a lion?" Troy said. "And he can wear our kit. He'll look so cool!"

"I do love your team spirit." Coach Reece smiled. "I think it's a great idea! I'll talk to the other coaches and see what we can do. We would be more than happy to pay for the mascot."

"No thanks, we've got this. We're doing the whole thing ourselves," Hassan added proudly.

Coach Reece laughed. "Okay, but we're here if you need us."

CHAPTER 15

Sounds Like A Plan

At the next training session, just before they had to start practice, Shay, Frankie, Oscar, Troy, Tandeep and Hassan huddled together to discuss the sponsored run.

"I can use my sister's computer to make a sponsor form and my mum can help me print it," said Oscar.

"I'll ask the other AC boys to help us," Hassan said, wanting to help, but not wanting to get involved with anything that required him to try to read anything. Reading wasn't one of his strong points.

"We can make posters and stick them up so that everyone knows about it and maybe we can give some to Tandeep and his dad so they can give them to everyone who gets in their taxi. Is that okay Tandeep?" asked Frankie.

The boys looked at Tandeep who shyly nodded. They were used to Tandeep being there but not contributing to the conversation. Tandeep was very shy. But he was a good footballer and that was all they cared about.

Tandeep looked down at the ground wanting to say something—anything! But he was afraid to say anything in case it came out all wrong and muddled.

"But *where* could we do the run?" Troy asked.

"I'll find somewhere," replied Shay.

"Okay cool and Hassan, remember, don't ask Jamie," said Troy.

"I think we should all get involved including Jamie. It's not up to you to decide who can and can't do it Troy," Hassan said.

Troy glared at him.

"That's true. It's our club so *all* of us should do it," Oscar said. "Hands up if you think everyone should do it."

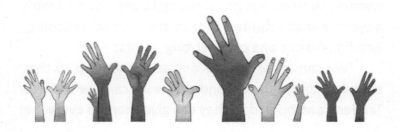

All the boys raised their hand and looked at Troy.

"Oh, shut up Oscar!" snarled Troy.

"Troy, just stop," Shay snapped.

"Fine, whatever." Troy crossed his arms moodily.

"Let's just ask everyone and it's up to them to decide if they want to do it," Frankie said.

Troy didn't answer. He continued to sulk with his arms crossed.

"Mum, me, Frankie and the boys from football are planning a sponsored run, so we can get some money to buy a club mascot. Can you help me find somewhere we can do it?"

"What a great idea! You could do it at the sports centre where I work. I'm sure they wouldn't mind."

"Can you take me there after school tomorrow please? I want to be the one to ask if we can use it," Shay said.

Joanne smiled. "Of course. I'm so proud of you lot. Where did you get the idea to do a sponsored run?"

"Oscar came up with it. I mentioned that you usually do the sponsored swims to raise money for Gran's charity and everyone freaked out saying they can't swim, so Oscar suggested we run instead."

"I love this idea, Shay. What can I do to help? I'm sure if we ask, the other parents will be happy to give us a hand."

"Well, actually Mum, we're planning the whole thing

by ourselves. We've all got different jobs to do and the team want to organise everything."

"Okay sweetheart, I'll take you to the sports centre tomorrow."

Shay ran up to his mum and wrapped his arms around her waist. "Thanks Mum."

CHAPTER 16

Three Weeks Until The Run

Over the next few weeks, Shay, Frankie and the rest of the under-nines worked hard to make the sponsored run a success.

Frankie and his mum made lots of posters with all the details of the run and gave them out to the players at the club. They put posters up around their local area in Islington including the library, Chapel Market, in some shop windows on the high street and in the Angel Centre.

Oscar's mums helped him make the sponsorship forms, which he gave out at training.

"Now, let's try to get as many sponsors as we can. We can start by asking our families and friends," Oscar said, as he handed out the sponsorship forms.

"I'll ask everyone that comes into my dad's restaurant," said Hassan.

"Make sure you don't let anyone leave until they

sponsor us!" Oscar winked at Hassan and everyone laughed.

"I'm going down to the fire station tomorrow to ask my dad's friends if they will sponsor us," said Frankie. "I'll try and leave one of the forms there so that people on the other shifts can do it as well."

"Great idea!" said Shay. "Oh, come on, Coach Joe's here."

At break time, while the boys were drinking their water, Shay and Frankie decided to try to speak to Jamie about the fun run. Jamie was playing by himself, doing roll overs with the football and cartwheels on the pitch.

"Jamie!" called Shay, trying to get his attention.

Jamie didn't respond. He carried on doing cartwheels and skipping around the field.

Jamie's mum, Kathy, noticed the boys trying to speak to Jamie and went over to see what the problem was.

"Hi boys," Kathy said. Her smile looked strained. "Has Jamie done something?"

Shay and Frankie glanced at each other.

"Oh no, Jamie hasn't done anything wrong. We're organising a sponsored fun run and we'd like Jamie to be part of it," Shay said.

"Oh," Kathy said with her eyes wide. "A fun run. . . and you'd like Jamie to join in?"

"Yep, we want to raise money to get a mascot for the

team. We're going to do a five-kilometre run," Frankie said.

Kathy began to smile; in fact, she almost began to cry. Nobody had ever invited her Jamie anywhere.

"I'm sure he'd love to be part of it," she eventually said.

"Good! We'll get him some posters and some sponsorship forms after training," Shay said.

As the boys walked away from Kathy, Shay turned back to look at Jamie, who had skipped over to his mum. He noticed Kathy hugging her son close and it looked as if she was wiping tears from her face.

At the end of training Coach Joe called the boys over.

"How's it all going with the sponsored run that I've been hearing so much about?"

"Things are going to plan," said Shay. "We even got Jamie involved."

"Oh well done!" Coach Joe said, giving the boys a high five. "Proud of you all."

CHAPTER 17

Countdown

"So far, I've filled in two sponsorship forms," said Hassan proudly.

"That's great!" said Frankie.

"Yeah, that's great," mocked Troy. "It's alright for you. You don't even have to do much to get sponsors. You just ask people that come into your restaurant."

"Troy give it a rest. That's the whole point. We all need to ask as many people as we can," said Oscar.

"Yeah I know but why's he showing off about it?"

"I'm not," Hassan said, holding up his hands. "I'm just saying."

"Everyone, let's just keep at it. Remember we're all in this together," said Oscar looking at the boys.

"I don't know why you're even saying anything Oscar. You're always late so you'll probably be so late you'll miss the whole thing!" shouted Troy.

"Guys stop!" Frankie said, and for a moment everyone was quiet.

"We've only got one week left to try and raise as much cash as we can, so let's not fall out now," Shay said, noticing Troy looking worried.

As soon as practice was over, Shay tapped Troy on the shoulder as he was grabbing his bag.

"Yeah?" Troy turned around.

"I wanted to check if you were okay about the run?"

"Why wouldn't I be? Why are you even asking me about the stupid run? I'm not even doing it!" Troy snapped.

"What? You have to do it. I thought you wanted to help out?"

"Well, things change and I'm not and no, I don't want to talk about it."

With his head down, Troy stormed off.

Shay caught Frankie's eye who mouthed, "What's up?" Shay held up his hand so Frankie would know to give him five minutes.

Shay ran after Troy. "What's wrong Troy? Maybe I can help?"

At first, Troy didn't answer and Shay almost left him

to it, but then Troy said. "If my mum was here, she'd help me to get sponsors. She'd take me out so I could ask people. My dad won't. He doesn't even get it."

"Where's your mum?"

"She travels back to Nigeria a lot, so it's just me, my dad and older brother. Dad doesn't care and my brother is too busy with uni. He doesn't even have time to come to church with us." Troy shrugged. "Sorry, I just miss my mum."

Shay couldn't imagine not seeing his mum every day. He thought about how lucky he was to have such a supportive family.

"When's she back?" Shay asked.

"I'm not sure but soon I hope."

"You mentioned church? Why don't you ask some of the people at your church to sponsor you?"

Troy thought for a moment then smiled. "That's a good idea. Thanks Shay."

"No worries. I better hurry back or my mum will be looking for me."

"You're a good mate, Shay," Troy said, and Shay beamed.

"See you later Troy." Shay waved as he hurried back to Frankie, who was patiently waiting for him. He felt good helping Troy with his problem.

"What was that all about?" Frankie asked, handing Shay his bag.

"I was just making sure Troy was okay but it's all good now. Race you to the car?"

"You're on!" Frankie said and the boys sprinted to where Tina and Joanne were waiting for them.

CHAPTER 18

The Day Of The Run

Three weeks later, AC United football team met at the local athletics club in Finsbury Park, ready to do the sponsored run, in front of their family and friends.

Shay and Frankie saw Coach Joe, Coach Kaan, Pete and some of the other coaches, but so far, no sign of Coach Reece.

The run was set to begin at midday, and as the time approached, Shay could see nearly everyone from the team. He smiled when he noticed Troy.

"Guys, look who's just turned up!" Troy laughed pointing towards the main entrance. As they looked over, Oscar came running in with minutes to spare.

Shay looked at Troy and pleaded with his eyes to leave Oscar alone but Troy couldn't help himself and burst out laughing. "Late again?"

"No wise cracks from you. I'm not in the mood," Oscar said.

It was time for the race to begin and as the boys began to make their way to the start line, they could already hear the encouraging voices from their families.

"Good afternoon. Is everyone ready?" shouted a very familiar voice over the megaphone.

Everyone turned to look in the direction of where the voice was coming from. Standing there, in his trademark red top and black tracksuit bottoms, was the legendary Coach Reece.

"Yes!" shouted the players and their families.

"It's a beautiful day for such a great event," he continued. "Now, parents and friends, let me hear you make some noise for AC United!"

The athletics club was filled with screams of "Go

on AC!" and "Good luck boys!" mixed with clapping, cheering and whistling.

"The run is about to begin. On your marks, get set, go!" Coach Reece yelled before he blew his whistle. The boys were off, arms and legs gliding through the air.

Jamie led the run to begin with but was soon overtaken by some of the older boys. The spectators were screaming and shouting, and this encouraged the boys to keep going.

Frankie was fast and kept up a good pace. He was up at the front with the older players, while Shay was in the middle, just behind Tandeep, but alongside Oscar. The spectators were clapping and cheering them along.

Suddenly, the cheering got louder and louder. Shay knew they must be near the finish line. As he looked ahead, he could see Frankie almost at the finish line.

"Go on, Frankie!" Shay panted under his breath.

Pushing ahead, Frankie crossed the finish line to screams from the spectators. He had won the race!

When the run was finally over, the boys were exhausted but it didn't stop them from giving each other high fives and congratulating Frankie on a great run.

Shay prayed that they had raised enough money to buy the mascot costume. The older boys came over to Frankie and congratulated him with fist bumps.

"Little man, you're really quick, even faster than us. I'm impressed!" said one of the older boys.

"Thanks," was all Frankie could manage to say. He couldn't stop smiling. In fact, he smiled so much he thought his face might get stuck.

Afterwards, to everyone's surprise, Frankie's dad and his mates turned up with their fire engine to hose down the boys. They had never felt so grateful to be cooled down.

"Can I ask you a few questions for the local newspaper?" a man, wearing glasses with a notepad and pen in his hands, asked Shay.

"Oh wow, sure," Shay said, wiping his sweaty brow.

"Tell me, how did you young boys come up with the idea of the sponsored run?"

"Well, it all started during break time at football practice. . ."

CHAPTER 19

Bring It On!

Training had been going very well since the sponsored run. Coach Reece sat them down at the beginning of the practice.

"I have some news for you." Coach Reece had the biggest smile on his face. "Firstly, we'd like to congratulate you for coming up with the idea to get a club mascot. We really loved that idea and, honestly, I can't believe we didn't have one already! Secondly, the way you worked together to raise the money made us very proud. We love your team spirit and hope you keep it up. You've raised enough money to buy the mascot costume and I believe it's been ordered!"

The boys cheered so loudly that Coach Reece had to cover his ears.

The sponsored run had brought them closer together. The boys were much sharper, faster and tighter and the coaches were pleased with their progress. So pleased, in fact, that Coach Joe told them that they would soon be ready to have a real match!

The boys were so excited at the thought of their first match of the season that all they could think about was training hard and getting ready.

A few weeks later, during a training session, Coach Reece was watching them and taking down notes. At the end of practice Coach Reece sat the boys down.

"Coach Joe tells me you're ready to compete in matches. What do you think?" teased Coach Reece.

"We're ready!" the boys shouted back.

Coach Reece laughed. "Well, in that case your first match is in two weeks and it'll be a friendly game against The Highbury Bears." Coach Reece had to speak louder over the boys' excited chatter. "Although it's a friendly, you're still expected to play as a team and go for a win."

Shay was excited but nervous. He knew of the Highbury Bears and they were a good team. In fact, some of the boys at his school played for them.

Shay leaned towards Frankie. "Sammy and Ben play for Highbury Bears. I'll be playing against our friends."

"Yeah, I know. Are you nervous? This won't be lunchtime football; this will be the real thing. They're really good as well. Do you think you're really up to it?"

Shay frowned. "Yeah, of course! Why would you ask me that?"

Frankie shrugged his shoulders.

"What's wrong with you Frankie? Don't say weird stuff like that just because I made the team and you didn't." Shay turned his back on his friend and shuffled closer to sit next to Hassan.

Frankie opened his mouth but no words came out. He knew it was true and didn't want to make things worse.

"Shay," Frankie eventually said and Shay glared at him. "I'm sorry and I bet you'll even score against the Bears."

"Thanks," Shay said frostily.

"Shay, on Monday when we're back at school, let's use our playtime and lunchtimes to practice some of the drills," Hassan suggested.

"Yeah cool."

"Can I practice with you as well?" asked Frankie.

Hassan hesitated. "Well. . . you're not on the team, so I thought it could be just the guys who are actually playing?"

"Cool," Frankie said getting up to walk away.

"No, look we can *all* train together," Shay stressed as Frankie walked away. "Frankie!"

"Forget it," Frankie called over his shoulder. He didn't want anyone to see that the tears were threatening to come.

"Frankie, wait up!" pleaded Shay but Frankie was moving further and further away.

Frankie looked for his mum and spotted her and Joanne talking to Coach Joe. His mum had his baby brother on her hip and was holding Katie's hand. As he got closer, he overheard Coach Joe telling his mum about the upcoming friendly game.

"The players only have three more training sessions before their first match, so everyone would need to be here on time for every session. Even those in the development squad."

"Do you think Frankie will get a chance to play?" Tina asked and Frankie held his breath.

"He's definitely improved, and boy is he fast, but to be honest it'll be the main team that play. Don't worry, he'll get his chance soon enough, but not this match."

Now the tears came and Frankie couldn't stop them. He hurried to his mum just as Coach Joe walked away.

"Can we go home now please?" Frankie asked. "I don't feel great."

He reached for his mum's hand and held onto it

tightly, something he hadn't done much of lately, forcing his little sister Katie to hold on to the pushchair.

"Of course, love," Tina said, looking at her son with concern. "See you later Joanne."

"Bye guys. Hope you feel better Frankie."

Frankie waved at Joanne without looking her in the eye.

CHAPTER 20

Three Is A Crowd

That evening, Shay couldn't stop thinking about Frankie. Even though he wasn't very kind earlier, he didn't want him to feel left out. He wanted to reassure him that he could join in the playtime training if he wanted to.

Just before bedtime Shay went to find his mum who was in the kitchen baking a cake.

"Mum, I know it's a bit late, but can I go on my computer and speak to Frankie please?"

Joanne glanced at the clock. "If you're quick. What's going on? Frankie said he wasn't feeling good."

Shay explained to his mum what happened at practice.

"Ah yes, I think it's worth having a chat," Joanne said, once she had heard the full story.

Two doors down at Frankie's house, after Tina had got the baby and Katie off to sleep, she went to find Frankie who was sitting alone on his bed, staring at a notification on his screen from Shay.

"Frankie, love, what's wrong? You haven't said a word since we left training." She placed a cool hand on his forehead. "And your temperature feels fine." Tina sat down on the bed and started stroking his hair.

Frankie rolled over onto his mum's lap, and as he began to tell her what had happened, tears filled his eyes, then slowly began to run down his cheeks.

"I just feel left out Mum. I want to play in the main team and I'm jealous that Shay gets to. What if he gets a new best friend? I think Hassan is trying to take him away from me. He's always leaving me out and I don't know why."

"Listen, don't worry, okay? Shay is still your best friend and he won't leave you out of anything. Look, he's trying to contact you," she said, noticing the notifications on the screen. "Just hear him out."

Tina kissed his forehead and once she was gone, Frankie put his headphones on.

"Frankie, are you alright?"

"Sorry again, Shay, for what I said earlier. It's just I

really want to play with you and it's obvious that Hassan doesn't like me."

"Forget him," Shay said. "You're so fast, I don't think anyone on the team is as fast as you, not even Hassan. I think he's a bit annoyed about that."

It had never occurred to Frankie that maybe Hassan was jealous of him.

"I just want to play with you again. I want us to be the dream team again."

"Frankie, of course we are. . . coming Mum. Look Mum's calling me but see you at school tomorrow and play football with us, yeah?"

"Yeah, okay. See you tomorrow."

Frankie smiled as he switched off his computer and put away his headphones.

The next morning, as Shay walked through the school gates and into the junior playground, Hassan was stood by the fence holding his football. His face lit up when he saw Shay.

"Hey, I brought my own ball in today so me and you can work on—"

"Have you seen Frankie?" Shay cut in. He looked around the playground for his best friend and waved when he spotted him. "There he is! Frankie!"

Frankie jogged over to them and couldn't help but notice the scowl on Hassan's face. Hassan deliberately turned around so his back was facing Frankie, blocking his view from Shay.

"Hassan, move man," groaned Shay stepping out of Hassan's way. "You're being rude."

"But I brought my ball in—"

"Can Frankie practice with us or not at break?" Shay asked. "If he can't then you can count me out."

Hassan shot Frankie a dark look and Frankie looked nervously back. "Fine, I don't know why you care. He's not even on the team." He turned to Frankie and with a blank face said, "See you at break," before walking off.

"Thanks for that," Frankie said just as the bell went for class.

"Of course! You're my best mate," Shay said, as they both walked to line up at their classroom door.

CHAPTER 21

King Of The Ring

"Hello boys," Coach Reece said. "Today I'm going to look at the under-nines, including the development squad. I'll be looking to see everyone's progress and decide who will play in the match."

Shay knew this meant that all the boys would have to up their game to try to impress him.

Frankie was feeling more and more confident about his skills. The coaches had been giving him lots of praise and he'd been doing some extra training with his dad. He knew today would be a good day to show off his skills.

Coach Joe stood next to Coach Reece with his hand on his hips and barked, "One lap round the pitch. Then I want you dribbling inside the marked-out area." He pointed to the area marked out by cones. "Using all parts of your feet, moving at different paces and using different ball skills!"

Once that was done Coach Reece said, "Now it's time for a game of number football. I'm going to shout out a number. When you hear it, leave your ball, run to the edge and complete five hurdle jumps. Make sure you finish and get back to your ball before I get to zero!"

As the boys continued dribbling around the area, using different turns, and parts of their feet, Coach Reece called out, "Ten!"

Everyone ran to the edge of the area, performed five hurdle jumps and got to their ball before he counted back to zero. After a few more turns of this, coach changed the drill. Next, it was a round of King Of The Ring.

Shay and Frankie grinned at each other. Training was always hard, but training like this made it fun.

"Let's see who the last boy standing will be. Who will be crowned King Of The Ring?"

Coach Reece blew the whistle and the game started immediately, with each boy trying to protect their own ball, while trying to kick their opponent's ball out of the 'ring.'

They were soon down to six players: Frankie, Tandeep, Hassan, Shay, Jamie and Tobias, a player from the development squad.

Hassan dodged in and out of the players protecting his ball skilfully, then kicked Tobias's ball out. Tobias ran out of the circle, and then there were five.

Jamie managed to manoeuvre around the edge of the circle keeping his ball close, then suddenly tackling Frankie and kicking his ball out of the ring. Next, Shay and Jamie went toe-to-toe, but neither boy got the better of each other. Suddenly, Shay switched towards Tandeep, skilfully tackling him while protecting his own ball, and it wasn't long before Tandeep was out.

Finally, they were down to the last three boys: Hassan, Jamie and Shay; each of them desperate to hang on to their ball.

As their teammates watched from the side lines, shouting out the name of the boy they wanted to win, Shay and Hassan's names could clearly be heard, no one seemed to be shouting for Jamie.

Jamie was good at this game. He was very focused and out of nowhere, Jamie kicked Shay's ball out of the ring. Disappointed, Shay ran off the pitch and stood around the edge as the other boys continued chanting for Hassan.

"Jamie! Jamie!" Shay began chanting and slowly the other boys began to join the chant with him. "Jamie! Jamie! Jamie!"

Jamie's mum, who was always at training, caught her breath when she realised the boys were cheering on her son. She hoped that her son was beginning to be accepted by the other boys.

From the corner of her eye, Kathy spotted Shay's mum. She had never spoken to her before. Actually, Kathy hadn't spoken to any of the parents. She took a deep breath and walked over.

"Hi, I'm Jamie's mum, Kathy," she said with her hand stretched out.

Joanne looked at her surprised. "I'm Joanne, Shay's mum."

"I know. I just wanted to say what a lovely young boy you have. He's been so nice to my Jamie."

"Thank you." Joanne smiled. "That makes me happy to hear that."

Jamie finally managed to tackle Hassan and kick his ball out to win the game and Coach Reece crowned Jamie King Of The Ring. Coach Reece held out his fist and Jamie bumped it with his own.

The session continued with a match between the team and the development squad, with each player doing their best to shine in front of their coaches.

When the over sixteens arrived for training, they stopped to watch the younger boys, cheering them on.

Towards the end of the session, the floodlights came on and the under-nines knew their training would soon be over. The floodlights were like an alarm clock, coming on at seven every evening.

When Coach Joe finally blew the whistle and signalled the end of training, Shay and his teammates threw themselves onto the ground in front of their Coach.

As usual, Jamie's mum brought over the tray of water bottles and the thirsty boys thanked her before drinking their water in big, fast gulps.

Coach Reece, Coach Joe and Coach Kaan huddled together talking in hushed voices.

Shay fell down on to the floor like a starfish, breathing hard. He was exhausted!

"Great session today guys," Coach Joe said, as Shay forced himself to sit up. "We saw some good skills and great team play. We were also impressed by the way you got behind Jamie when we played King Of The

Ring. You also have some money left over from the sponsored run and it's up to you to decide what you want to do with it."

Frankie put his hand up.

"Yes Frankie?" Coach Joe said.

"Shay came up with the idea of the mascot and raising money. I think he should decide."

"Yeah," Troy agreed. "That's a good idea."

All the other boys agreed too and Shay couldn't hide his surprise.

"Oh wow, thanks everyone. Err. . . if it's okay it would be cool to donate it to the charity that helped my grandma. That's where I got the raising money idea from."

"What charity is that Shay?" asked Coach Reece.

"It's one that helps people with Leukaemia. They helped us learn how to look after my grandma and stuff like that. I can't remember the name of the charity but I can ask Mum."

"That's a great idea," Coach Reece said. "Everyone in favour, raise your hands."

All of AC United raised their hands.

"Then that's decided," said Coach Reece. "Oh, and before I forget, it would be good if all of you can come to the match to support each other."

Frankie prayed he would get at least a few minutes playing in the actual game.

CHAPTER 22

Eyes R Us

That evening, after training, Coach Reece and Coach Joe stayed behind for a chat about the players and the upcoming match. They talked about the boys on the team and those in the development squad.

"We definitely have some good players coming through in the development squad," Coach Reece said.

"Frankie could be such a great player if only his passing and interceptions were better," Coach Joe sighed.

"Well, I'm glad you mention Frankie, because I think I might know why his aim isn't on target," Coach Reece said. "I'm going to call his mum. I think getting his eyes checked will make a huge difference."

Tina's mobile rang loudly from the dining table. With

her baby asleep in her arms, she quickly answered it hoping it wouldn't wake him up.

"Hello? Oh, hi Coach Reece. We're all fine, thanks." Tina was quiet for a while before replying. "I see. Thanks Coach, we'll look into it. Thank you. Okay, good night." She hung up the phone.

Although Tina was glad that Coach Reece might have noticed something about Frankie, she felt disappointed with herself and Colin that they hadn't spotted it themselves.

Tina used her phone to search for the number of Eyes R Us on Google to make an appointment for Frankie to have his eyes tested.

Tina searched her jeans pocket and found a clean tissue, which she used to wipe her eyes as the tears began to fall. She wasn't crying because Frankie might need to wear glasses, but because she hadn't noticed that he might need to.

*

The following day after school, Colin took his son to the opticians for an eye test. While Colin filled out forms and spoke to the optician, Frankie walked around looking at the glasses on display. He didn't like the look of any of them and hoped his eyesight was just fine. He couldn't imagine having to wear glasses.

How can I play football while wearing glasses?

Frankie sighed and sat down next to his dad. Just as he was improving at football, he felt like the glasses would set him back.

"Don't look so worried," said the optician. "You and Dad come with me. I'm just going to check your eyes with a sight test. It won't hurt."

Frankie sat on a big chair in the middle of the room with his dad close by. First, the optician asked Frankie to read the letters on an eye chart, which started out quite big, then got smaller and smaller as they went down the page.

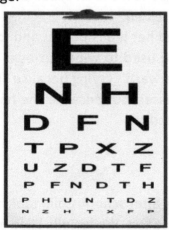

Next, the optician shone a bright light into each of Frankie's eyes for a moment to see how his pupils reacted.

Then, the optician moved his finger in front of

Frankie's eyes in different directions to check how Frankie's eyes followed it.

"Okay Frankie, we're all done. You are what we call short-sighted. That's why things you look at in the distance appear blurred and not very clear."

Frankie stared glumly at the floor as the optician kept talking.

"Dad tells me you're a keen footballer. Is that right?"

Slowly and without looking up, Frankie nodded his head.

"When you play football do you have some difficulty seeing players when they're in the distance or seeing a target?" continued the optician.

Again, Frankie nodded his head without looking up.

"Then come with me. I have exactly what you need."

The optician led Colin and Frankie over to a shelf that Frankie hadn't bothered to look at earlier. The shelf was full of smaller glasses in a range of colours. Although Frankie was slightly more hopeful, he was certain they wouldn't stay on during football and that they'd fall off and he'd be left feeling embarrassed. It would give Hassan something else to say about him.

The optician opened a drawer and pulled out two pairs of glasses: one bright red and one bright blue. He held them out to Frankie.

"Take a look at these and tell me what you think," said the optician.

Frankie looked at the blue pair and noticed it had a strap on it.

"These are our special wrap-around sports glasses for people who do sports like football. No chance of them falling off when you're playing! And look how stylish they are." The optician winked at Frankie.

Frankie took them and turned them over and over in his hands looking at them doubtfully. He looked up at his dad and slowly handed him the pair of glasses without saying a word.

"Did you know that lots of famous footballers like Wayne Rooney, Kaká, Edgar Davids and Ian Wright wear glasses?" said the optician.

"Ian Wright?" Frankie quizzed his dad.

Wrighty was one of Frankie and Shay's heroes. He used to play for Arsenal (their stadium wasn't far from their homes) and they loved to listen when he commentated on a match. Wrighty often got emotional when watching a match and the boys thought he was hilarious.

"Yes son, Ian Wright, Wright, Wright!" Colin sang making Frankie smile. "Come on Frankie, try them on. They look really good."

Frankie tried the glasses on and agreed they looked. . . okay. The optician spoke to Colin and said they could have them ready for collection on Thursday. Just in time for school on Friday.

CHAPTER 23

Footballers Wear Glasses Too!

On Friday, Frankie took the glasses to school in his book bag. Yesterday, when he and Colin had arrived home from the opticians, Frankie had put his glasses on and worn them around the house. His mum and sister told him he looked great, and Frankie didn't hate them, but today was different. This was school and he was worried what his friends might say.

On the way to school he walked with Shay and showed him the glasses.

"Wow Frankie! They look cool. Why don't you put them on?"

But Frankie just shook his head and put them back into his book bag. He wasn't quite ready.

Just before the whistle blew to start the school day, Tina had gone over to speak to Mrs Anderson, Frankie's teacher, about his new glasses—she wanted to explain that he was feeling embarrassed about wearing them.

Mrs Anderson, who herself wore glasses, smiled reassuringly at Tina. "Don't you worry, you leave it with me."

A few minutes later, once the children were seated and the register had been taken, Mrs Anderson walked over to the board and rubbed off what she had planned. Instead, she wrote on the board 'Famous People Who Wear Glasses.'

"Right children, I would like you spend just five minutes writing down any famous person you know who wears glasses."

Some of the children looked confused at each other. Sarah, who always asked questions, raised her hand but Mrs Anderson shook her head.

"I'll explain why later. Please begin writing."

Frankie decided to write about famous footballers that wore glasses. After five minutes, Mrs Anderson asked the class to stop writing.

"Is there anyone who would like to share their work?"

Ade put her hand up and went first. She spoke about a musician called Will.i.am. Melek was next and she had written about Harry Potter. Mrs Anderson laughed and reminded Melek that they were supposed to write about real people, not fictional characters. Then, Frankie put his hand up. Mrs Anderson nodded at him and Frankie cleared his throat.

"Wayne Rooney, Kaká, Edgar Davids and Ian Wright are all professional footballers, and they all wear glasses. I have a picture here of Davids and he wears glasses with straps on, called wrap arounds, when he's playing."

Sarah immediately put her hand up. "That can't be true. If you played football, your glasses wouldn't stay on."

Frankie felt his cheeks go warm. "Well, actually Sarah, there are sports glasses that footballers can wear that do stay on and they're really cool." He took the glasses out of his bag and held them up for everyone to see. "These glasses have been specially designed for people who play sports like football. This strap goes around the back of your head and helps to hold your glasses in place."

Tom, who had always worn glasses and had lost and broken many, walked over to Frankie. "Can I have a look?"

"Sure," Frankie said handing them over.

"These are cool! I'm going to ask my mum if I can get some."

"I got them at Eyes R Us on the high street. They come in red as well."

Instead of putting his glasses back into his book bag, Frankie decided to put them on.

"They really suit you," Mrs Anderson said. "I might get a pair for myself so I can play football." She winked and the class laughed.

At playtime Shay ran outside to start a football game. As the boys picked their sides, Shay looked around to find Frankie, but he was nowhere to be seen.

Frankie was still in the classroom and hadn't moved from his seat. Mrs Anderson was wiping the board and almost jumped when she noticed Frankie.

"Frankie, what are you doing still sitting there? You're missing playtime." Frankie looked up at his teacher but didn't answer. "Are you worried about something?"

"No," Frankie said in a small voice. "It's my glasses."

"What about them?" Mrs Anderson asked.

"I know the strap is meant to hold them in place but what if they break? What if I fall flat on my face and break them?"

"Oh dear," Mrs Anderson said. "Right, stand up." Frankie stood. "Spin around, jump up and down, touch your toes."

Frankie did all of it even though he was confused as to why.

"You see! The glasses haven't moved once. They are secure and will work just fine."

Frankie touched his glasses. She was right. They were in the exact same place. "Thanks Mrs Anderson."

"You're welcome. Now you don't have long left of playtime," she said as she gently guided him out of the classroom door. "I'm sure your friends are waiting for you."

Frankie ran outside and spotted the group of boys playing football.

"Frankie!" Shay called before passing him the ball.

Frankie ran for it and caught it on the shoulder, dropping the ball to his feet, before passing it to one of his friends.

The frantic game continued and not once did Frankie's glasses move. As the whistle blew to signal the end of playtime there was a sudden roar of, "Goal!"

Frankie had made the perfect pass to Shay, who neatly tucked the ball into the top right-hand corner of the goal, a perfect 'Top Bin.'

As the friends walked over to line up to go back to class, Frankie and Shay fist bumped each other.

"That was a great pass," Shay said to him.

Frankie gave him a thumbs up. Nobody, not even Hassan, commented on his glasses.

That evening, Shay and Frankie were playing FIFA on the computer.

"Frankie, are you coming to the match tomorrow? I'm sure my dad will pick you up if you want to come."

"I'm not sure. Me and my dad have been doing some extra training, so I think I'll see if he's free to take me over the park to do a bit more tomorrow," Frankie said.

It was partly true. Frankie thought training with his dad would distract him from not playing tomorrow.

"But Frankie," Shay stressed. "Coach said it would be good for everyone to come, even if they're not playing, and I really want you there."

"I know but. . ."

"You'll get to play a match soon," Shay said. "I need my best mate there."

"Okay, I'll be there. I promise. What time?"

"We've got to be at Highbury Fields for ten, so make sure you're ready early. I don't want to be late."

"Will do. And Shay?"
"Yeah?"
"You'll be great. I'll cheer you on," Frankie said.
"Thanks mate." Shay beamed.

CHAPTER 24

3 - 2 - 1 UNITED!

"Come on, Dad! Don't forget we're picking up Frankie. He's coming to watch the match," Shay said, as he pulled on his favourite football boots.

"FREEZE! Take those boots off and put them on when you get there," Joanne said with her hands on her hips.

"But Mum—" Shay was interrupted by a quick tickle to the head by Danny. "Dad. Stop!" Shay laughed.

He put his hands up to protect his head and Danny swooped down and whipped the hanging football boots from his son's feet.

"We don't want boot marks all over the new carpet. We won't hear the last of it," Danny whispered to Shay.

He was right. Shay didn't want to feel the wrath of his mum!

Today's match was a friendly game. AC United versus Highbury Bears and it would be played on the Bears' home pitch.

Saturday morning traffic in Highbury was usually bad so Danny, Joanne, Shay, Rayne and Frankie set off early to make sure they wouldn't be late. Shay could barely sit still in the car. He was so excited!

They arrived in plenty of time and walked over to Coach Joe and Coach Kaan who were surrounded by the other footballers.

"Morning all. Let's have a great match," Coach Joe said clapping his hands. "Get your football boots on and make your way to the pitch to get warmed up."

"Will the mascot be here today?" Oscar asked.

Coach Kaan shook his head. "Hopefully it should arrive by next week."

"Shay, hold your bag for a minute, while I tighten your laces." Danny bent down to tie up Shay's boots. "Don't forget to create space for yourself. Keep your head up and look out for Tandeep and Oscar, your midfielders. And don't forget to call for the ball, okay?"

Shay nodded. Danny gently squeezed his son on the shoulder and winked at him. "Good lad. Off you go and have fun!"

"Good luck Shay!" added Frankie, patting his friend on the back.

"Right boys, over here please!" called Coach Joe using his large hand to wave them over to him. "Let's get started. Over there and do one lap around that field."

Coach Joe pointed to a large open space and the players jogged over to begin their warm-up. Coach Joe followed it with his usual stretches and by the end the players were ready.

Just at the end of the warm-up, Coach Reece arrived. He called the boys over.

"If you play like we've seen you playing recently, you'll be fine. We're looking forward to this game so have fun and just enjoy yourselves. As Hassan was captain last season and a good leader, he'll stay as captain for today's match. Now close your eyes and breathe deeply. Remember a practice where you played particularly well and remember how you felt on the day. Now replay in your mind what you did well. Was it a good shot? An excellent tackle? Or maybe an out of this world save?" He waited a beat. "Now open your eyes and share what you're going to do today to help your team."

"I'll use my height to jump and get the ball away from the goal," Hassan said.

"I'll peel off the defender and get myself into spaces so I can receive the ball and score," Shay said.

"I'll keep moving and play quickly," Blessing added.

"Apart from trying to save goals, I'll keep communicating with the defenders," Maxwell said.

"Tandeep?" questioned Coach Reece hoping for an answer. Tandeep didn't answer, so Coach said, "You, know what to do? Stop attacks."

Tandeep nodded.

"Oscar, and you?" Coach Reece asked.

"Get that ball to Shay or try and score myself."

"And Jamie?" he asked.

Jamie began scratching his head and rubbing his face. He quickly looked at everyone staring at him, then back at Coach. He'd forgotten what Coach had asked him. Patiently, Coach Reece asked him again and this time Jamie simply replied, "Defend."

As the players finished sharing what they were going to do, the Highbury Bears appeared from behind them wearing luminous orange shirts and black shorts. As they slowly jogged on to the pitch, they looked confident, very confident.

Most of their players seemed taller than AC United. *They really needed a quick growth spurt!* Joanne thought when she saw the other team.

But there was no time for growing—it was time to play football.

CHAPTER 25

The Match

At every friendly match it was usual for the home team to use a parent that knew a bit about football to referee the game. Today it was the turn of a rather excited dad who was dressed in an adult-sized Bears football top and black shorts. Around his neck hung a long lanyard with a shiny whistle dangling on the end. He had the biggest smile the boys had ever seen. Shay and the others were pleased to see a friendly-looking Ref.

Walking along the edge of the pitch, the Bears' club secretary was a very tall man—almost as tall as Coach Joe. He was wearing a Bears football top and had a mobile phone in his hand. He was looking around as if searching for a good position to stand in. He would be the commentator for the match and his voice recording would be written up as the commentary for the game. It would be in the community sports section of the local newspaper.

The Ref called the captains over. Hassan stepped forward, nodded at his team and jogged over.

Shay glanced at his parents and best friend in the crowd. Frankie cupped his hands around his mouth and shouted, "Good luck Shay!"

His dad gave him a smile and a thumbs up, while his mum gave him a wave. Feeling more confident that he had such great support in the crowd, he felt focused and ready.

"Here comes the captain of AC United, Hassan, joined by Ted, the Bears captain," the commentator announced. "Look at all the players on their toes in their starting positions, ready to go. The Ref is going to ask the visiting team to make the call, so what'll it be from Hassan: heads or tails? The Ref is doing the toss aaaaand. . . oooh! The Bears win it. The teams are ready, so on the Ref's whistle."

The whistle blew.

Except for the goalies, all the players began running towards the ball. The spectators were shouting encouragement and the coaches were closely observing every move, calling out instructions to their teams.

"Just listen to that crowd! The Bears captain takes a shot at goal. . . oooh, it hits the post."

"Unlucky!" shouted one of the Bears' parents.

The game quickly began to move to the other end of the pitch. Shay could hear the commentator in the background as he ran to follow Jamie to the ball.

"Excellent dribbling from AC's Jamie and what great control. Jamie passes the ball to AC captain Hassan, the ball is quickly intercepted by Lucas from the Bears, and the game is moving back to the other end of the pitch. . . AC United are falling behind. . . and the Bears' number seven scores!"

"Ah man!" Shay groaned.

The Bears cheered and hugged surrounding their number seven player.

"Keep your heads up, boys! Keep going!" Jamie's mum shouted.

"Maxwell, the goalie for AC, is stretching the ball above his head, and he throws it to Tandeep, who's in the clear. Tandeep quickly dribbles towards the Bears goal and passes to Shay."

Shay could hear his mum shouting, "Go on boy!" from the crowd.

"Shay tackles both the Bears' captain and number eleven at the same time! He's keeping control of the ball, look at him go! He's racing towards the goal!"

All Shay could hear was, "Go Shay! Go Shay!" He curled the ball past the keeper and into the top right-hand corner.

"GOOOOAL!" yelled the commentator and the crowd roared. The AC team surrounded Shay and hugged him.

"Come on!" shouted an excited Frankie, as he ran along the pitch in and out of the parents, following the ball as the teams kept going. He wished he was part of the game but watching his friends play was way more fun than he thought it would be.

"Some brilliant saves from both goalies here, quick substitutions and some great passes between the players all around. Oh, wait, look here, keep an eye on the AC Captain, look at him go, Hassan takes a shot but the goalie blocks it with his foot. Ooh, bad luck! Hang on! Where did number ten come from? Wow! Shay's run straight past the keeper and hit it to the back of the net. Fantastic work. His second goal of the match."

The AC parents went wild when Shay's second goal went in. His team mates quickly ran over to Shay to congratulate him.

The game continued with two more goals scored by the Bears, and although AC were playing well, the Bears were still in front. By half time it was three goals to two to the Bears.

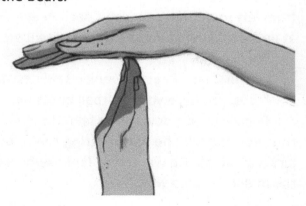

During the half time break, the coaches sat the players down to rest their legs and drink lots of water.

"You're doing great boys," Coach Reece said as Shay took a puff from his inhaler. "Remember to do what you've practised in training. Take possession of the ball and keep moving it forward. If we don't have possession it becomes everyone's job to defend."

"What's wrong, Oscar?" asked Maxwell.

Oscar was one of the midfielders and he was holding his tummy. His face had turned a strange grey colour.

Coach Joe took him to the side, then after a quick chat, led him to a bench.

Shay watched as Coach Joe, Coach Kaan, Coach Reece and Pete huddled together and was surprised to see they kept glancing at Frankie. Shay crossed his fingers.

Please ask Frankie to play, he prayed.

Coach Reece walked over to Frankie. Frankie looked from left to right to see who Coach Reece was staring at and it took him a moment to realise it was him!

"Hi Frankie."

"Err hi Coach Reece," Frankie said nervously.

"I see you have your football boots on."

Frankie looked down at his feet. His mum had asked this morning why he was wearing them, but Frankie just wanted to. He wanted to feel like he was part of the match in some way.

"Oscar's not feeling very well and we need a midfielder. I know you're not part of the main team yet, but we'd like to use you as a sub today, what do you think? Can you step in and replace Oscar?"

"Oh wow! Yes please," Frankie said excitedly.

"Amazing! I've been watching you running alongside the pitch, so I know you're warmed up. Let me grab you a kit," Coach Reece said walking to his bag.

Frankie ran over to Shay's parents with the biggest grin. "I get to play! Coach Reece has just asked me to sub!"

"Oh love, that's amazing!" Joanne said hugging him tight. "I'm going to record it all for your mum and dad."

"Knock 'em dead," Danny said, giving Frankie a high five.

Frankie grinned and ran over to the team. Shay's eyes widened the closer he got before he shouted a massive, "YESSSS!" and ran to Frankie, grabbing him in a hug.

Coach Reece laughed. "Alright boys, save that energy for the match. Put this on Frankie."

He handed him an AC top.

CHAPTER 26

A Game Of Two Halves

"It's the second half, folks! And wow, we're off to a good start. The boys are really chasing that ball across the pitch! Look at that dribbling, some nice tackling there, and oh no! We have an injury! Sammy, number nine from the Bears, has accidentally been hit in the face by the ball. It looks like he'll have to come off!

"Now we're into the last three minutes of the match and all the boys are trying to get a goal for their team! Troy passes to Hassan. Hassan's running down the middle of the pitch with the ball, while. . . who's that? He's got a keen dad running along the edge of the pitch alongside him!"

It was Hassan's dad shouting something in Turkish.

"Hassan has lost the ball but Frankie, the sub for AC who replaced Oscar, has won it back! Frankie passes it back to Hassan and look at that focus. Will Hassan take the shot?"

The AC parents were shouting and willing him on. Hassan set his sights, focused, and took the shot.

"And the ball flies over the goalie's hands! Straight into the back of the net and it's another goal for AC United!"

"GOOOOOAL!" screamed the AC players.

In no time it was the last minute of the game and the score was now three all. It was raining but no one seemed to care. The parents were too busy cheering on their kids, while the coaches were shouting instructions. The atmosphere was electric.

"And it's the AC captain, Hassan, running down the pitch. Several Bears players try to tackle him but, sorry Bears, Hassan isn't stopping! He dribbles the ball across the pitch. Oh no, he's been stopped by the Bears' number four. Hassan's fallen to the floor. I think he might be injured."

The Ref blew the whistle and the game came to an abrupt stop. Everyone fell silent.

The AC players ran over to see if their captain was okay; Hassan was holding his ankle, writhing in agony.

The boys stepped back to give the Ref some room. He crouched down beside Hassan.

The Bears were standing around waiting patiently but their number four was staring at Hassan and smirking. Troy noticed and marched over to him.

"Oi, that was a foul!" shouted Troy. "You did that on purpose to stop him scoring. That should be a penalty!"

As the rest of the AC team began to agree with Troy, Shay turned to the Ref.

"Ref, that was a penalty," Shay argued.

Some of the AC parents joined in shouting out, "Foul!"

"Let me sort out this young man first," the Referee said. He helped Hassan to his feet.

"I can still play," Hassan said and the Referee looked at him doubtfully. "It's manageable. Please Ref!"

"Okay, but if it starts to hurt more you have to let me know." The Referee blew his whistle and walked over to the Bears' number four player. He flashed him a yellow card and the AC team cheered.

"Wait, wait, what will it be? Yes, it looks like it's a free kick to AC," the commentator continued.

"It should be a penalty," Shay moaned.

"Yeah Ref!" Frankie said.

"We deserve a penalty," Troy shouted.

"Guys, play on!" Coach Kaan yelled. "Troy take the shot!"

"The ball is tossed to Troy, who quickly gets

into position and takes the shot, but it's wide," the commentator said. "And the Ref is looking at his watch. The whistle has blown. It's a draw, the final score is three all."

The parents clapped, cheered and shouted congratulations as the players shook hands and the coaches and Referee did the same.

The AC coaches called the under-nines over for a post-match team talk.

"Guys, sit down for a minute," Coach Joe said. The players sat on the grass in front of their coaches. "You were awesome today. Each and every one of you played your part. On your own, you're all good players, but as a team you're awesome. Well done Frankie. You made your mark today and coming on as a sub without warning. That was a great pass you made to assist Hassan with that goal, and Hassan well done for finishing the game."

The players immediately jumped up and began patting Frankie on the back to congratulate him, all except Hassan. Hassan wouldn't admit that Frankie had become a good player. He hoped Frankie didn't become a better player than him.

"I can see there's going to be some great Baller Boys coming out of this team soon," added Coach Reece. "We have a packed-out season ahead and I'm excited to see you all play some great matches. We've just had word from the Bears that they've chosen Shay as player of the match. Well done number ten."

The coaches and the team gave Shay a huge clap.

"We also have a rematch next weekend against the Bears, so you'll get your chance to really show them what winners you are."

"Yes!" the boys cheered.

"Come on then, right hand in." Coach Reece held out his hand.

All the players, and their coaches, put their right hand in the middle, on top of each other, and Coach Reece shouted, "Three. . . two. . . one!"

The boys threw their hands in the air and shouted, "UNITED!"

Chapter 27
Team Spirit

The friendly against the Highbury Bears had been a good start for the AC United's under-nines team. The parents were proud of how well their sons had played and the coaches were impressed with how brilliantly the boys had played as a team. The boys were just relieved that they hadn't lost the match!

The AC parents were smiling and chatting to each other. Jamie's mum, Kathy, was too busy keeping an eye on Jamie to talk to the other parents. Joanne saw her and went over.

"Hi! Just wanted to say how well your son played today. He's really good."

"Oh, thank you, Joanne. Jamie loves his football,

and this club is the best thing that's ever happened to him," Kathy said. "I'm sure you've noticed he's a bit lively? He has ADHD and bringing him here to AC has been great for all of us. The coaches are brilliant with him, really patient, and my Jamie loves his football. I must say, your son is one of the only players on the team that has ever made an effort to be friendly towards him."

"Oh thank you. Shay thinks Jamie is a great player," Joanne said.

As the two mums looked over at Jamie, he was throwing stones up into the air without thinking about where they might land.

"Excuse me," said Kathy, running towards Jamie.

Shay was standing with his dad, who handed him his inhaler and spacer.

"Well done, boy. You were great today. I'm so proud of you! Making player of the match in your first game, what an achievement! And you, Frankie, stepping in and helping the team to victory!"

"Thanks." Frankie grinned, looking down on what he now thought of as his lucky football boots.

"Dad, did you hear what Coach Reece said?" Shay jumped up and down. "He said there's going to be some great Baller Boys coming out of this team."

"Amazing!" Danny said, hugging Shay. "I have no doubt he was talking about you and Frankie."

"And, he said our next match is next week against the Bears."

"I hope I get to play again," Frankie said. "I had so much fun!"

"I'm so proud of you two," Joanne said, hugging both the boys.

"Frankie?" They all turned to see Coach Reece. "Let me take a look at those super glasses."

Frankie took them off. Coach Reece held them up high to the light.

"They seem to have done the trick. Your passing today was right on target. Keep this up and I'm sure you'll make the main team. Well done mate."

"Thanks Coach. I can't wait," replied Frankie.

Shay walked over, just as Coach Reece headed off to

speak to Jamie and his mum. Shay put his arm around his best friend's shoulder.

"You'll make the team, Frankie. You were really good. Do you think your glasses helped?"

Frankie thought for a moment, then said, "You know what? When I was on the pitch, I forgot I was wearing them! I was just getting on with playing football, but the straps are brilliant! My glasses didn't fall off and I was worried that they would. When I passed the ball to Hassan and he scored, I saw the ball hit the back of the net so clearly. It was wicked!"

As the two friends happily chatted away, Hassan came limping over.

"Hey guys, I thought I'd bring my ball in on Monday so the three of us can practice."

To their surprise, Hassan slung his arm over Frankie's shoulder.

"Really?" Frankie frowned.

Shay looked at them both and laughed. "Hassan, is there something you want to say to Frankie?"

Hassan smiled. "Yeah, I was going to say thanks for setting me up with that goal. You were on point."

"Oh anytime," Frankie said. He couldn't hide his surprise that Hassan had paid him a compliment.

Hassan held out his fist and Frankie bumped his own against it. They watched as Hassan limped over to his family.

"Right you two, come on, let's go. Frankie, I bet you can't wait to tell your dad about today can you?" Danny grinned.

"He'll be so happy!" Frankie said. "And I can't wait for training on Friday to see who they pick for the match."

The two friends put their arms across each other's shoulders as they walked towards the car.

CHAPTER 28

Let's Play Football!

Hassan had been absent from school all week, and when he didn't turn up for training on Friday, Shay and Frankie knew something was wrong; Hassan never missed training.

"Right guys, before we get started, I have a bit of news. Last weekend at the match against the Bears, Hassan's injury resulted in him having a badly sprained ankle and the doctors have told him he needs to rest it. Unfortunately, this means he won't be able to play in the match tomorrow."

The players looked shocked and disappointed, as not only was Hassan their friend, but he was also their captain and a good player. They needed him.

"Don't worry, he'll be back with us in no time but in the meantime we will need a new captain." Coach Joe looked at the players, his eyes stopping on Shay. "And that's going to be Shay."

"Really?" Shay asked with his eyes wide. He couldn't believe it! "Thanks Coach."

"You played great Shay. Now I'm going to read out whose playing tomorrow. Shay, Oscar, Blessing, Frankie—."

"Yes!" shouted Frankie, jumping in the air, before Coach Joe had even finished.

Coach Joe cleared his throat and Frankie blushed.

"Sorry Coach. I'm just so excited."

Coach Joe laughed. "I can see that mate. Where was I? Troy, Tandeep. . ."

But Frankie wasn't paying any attention. He had done it! He caught Shay's eye and they grinned at each other.

The game would be played on AC United's turf, Marshals Playing Fields. Luckily, Colin wasn't working so would be going to the match with Frankie.

As they walked across the grass, Shay and his family were already there. Frankie ran over to join them. The atmosphere was lively. As it was a home game lots of the older AC players turned up early to support the under-nines before their own games later in the day. Pete was there in his AC top, with his clipboard, pen and phone, ready to write the commentary on the game to send to the local paper.

As Shay and Frankie walked over to join the rest of the team, they noticed that Tandeep was standing with his dad.

"Tandeep, walk over with us," Shay suggested.

Tandeep looked at his dad, who waved him on, then, without saying anything joined the boys. His dad smiled watching his son interact with the other children.

As most of the under-nines gathered and sat around Coach Reece and Coach Kaan, the Highbury Bears arrived with their supporters.

"Look at them. They think they're so good," snarled Troy, "Well, this game is ours!" He shouted in their direction.

"Okay, let's see who we've got here," said Coach Kaan scanning the players. "Anyone seen Oscar?"

"He's always late, but he'll come," Blessing said and the boys laughed.

"Where's Coach Joe? Is he not here yet?" Oscar asked. He had quickly slipped in amongst the others, acting like he'd been there the whole time.

Coach Kaan rolled his eyes and the boys giggled.

The players and their families fell silent to hear what the Coaches were about to say, but they were distracted by something in the distance.

"Look!" yelled Rayne pointing in the direction of the club house. Everyone turned. For a moment the players and parents were silent then erupted into loud cheers. In the distance stood a large, fluffy lion and it was wearing an AC United football kit!

The under-nines quickly ran in the direction of their new mascot, with their family and friends following behind them. As they got closer the mascot began to shake its hips and wave its paws in the air. It was dancing!

The mascot made its way over to the under-nines team and shook all their hands, then wiggled its bottom and took a bow. The crowd laughed and clapped with excitement.

"This is so cool," Shay said.

"Very cool," Frankie agreed.

The funny thing was nobody seemed to know who was wearing the costume until it began to rap.

"It's Coach Joe, Coach Joe!" they all began to shout.

The mascot danced and pranced and wiggled its bottom one more time, before slowly lifting off its head.

"Surprise! Blimey, it's hot in here and I'm too old for all this dancing around." Coach Joe unzipped the front of the costume. "You'll need to sort yourselves out a permanent mascot, as this is a total one off from me!"

"Coach you were good, but not that good!" joked Oscar.

"I'd like to see you in this!" Coach Joe laughed, nudging Oscar gently with the lion head.

"Right guys, the fun's over for now," Coach Reece said clapping his hands. "We have a game to play."

Shay and the boys searched out the opposition, looking for number four who had injured Hassan. They spotted him, chatting and laughing with his mates, as if he hadn't done anything wrong. The AC boys glared at him.

"I should go over and have a word with him!" Troy said.

"Hey! None of that," Coach Reece said. "You save that energy for the game."

"You're right Coach. Come on guys, let's win this for Hassan," Shay said.

BALLER BOYS

"For Hassan!" the boys chorused.

"That's more like it!" Coach Reece smiled. "Let's play some football!"

"This book is about more than football, it's about people. Young people and their possibilities. Venessa Taylor has a fresh, unique approach to writing. She is a true creative. Every character is whole, and this book has soul."
Professor Benjamin Zephaniah

About the Author

Venessa Taylor brings two decades of experience as an inner-city primary school teacher and assistant headteacher to the creation of the Baller Boys series. Aimed at encouraging young children to enjoy reading, the football-themed stories are written with young readers, especially boys, in mind. Born and raised in London, Venessa continues her legacy as a literacy lead through her stories.

Please share your reviews and Baller Boys photos on Twitter @VenessaTwrites
and
www.ballerboysbooks.com